ASSASSIN'S

GAMBIT

THE BIG BAD WOLF HAS A NEW MISSION—PROTECT THE PRINCESS—
EVEN IF IT COSTS HIM EVERYTHING

ELLE BEAUMONT

Published by Crescent Sea Publishing.
www.crescentseapublishing.com

Cover designed by Cover A Day.
www.coveraday.com

For anyone who has ever felt like their back is against the wall
—keep on fighting—we all have a little warrior inside of us.

CHAPTER 1

IN HINDSIGHT, I should have brought Raif with me to the castle's ball, and I should have scouted the area better beforehand, but I didn't, and now the king's assassin was getting away. This was not how I expected the night to go.

The masked woman glided down the rope and vanished into the dark of the night. Below the balcony, guards stood at their post, still unaware of what transpired. It wouldn't be long until they discovered their king was dead. I grunted, slithering downward. I had to give it to the masked demoness: she was fast.

I leapt from the rope and onto the ground, chasing after the fading figure. She discarded her dress slippers and ran at the wall. Just as we both approached it—as my fingers were just about to yank onto the fabric of her dress—she scurried up the wall and over onto the other side. Cursing beneath my breath, I pursued her and flopped onto the other side.

There is a saying: *look before you leap*. It is wise to listen to it, and in this case, I didn't. At the base of the wall, a cloud of smoke met me. Thick and dark, it clung to my nostrils and my eyes. The only thing I heard was the woman's laughter and her voice. I snarled, unable to fumble out of the cloud. It stung my eyes and my nose. I hadn't been prepared and because of that, I failed.

"It has been fun. I look forward to our future dances, but I really must be on my way." Hoofbeats replaced the sound of her voice, and soon the roar of the guards blared behind us.

I hacked, coughing, and wheezing as I collapsed to my knees. Crawling was my only option to get away from the gas that threatened to choke me out. With a reddened face, I sucked in a glorious breath of fresh, clean air.

Not a moment later, a guard rushed around the wall, and saw me hunched over. He grabbed my arm roughly, hoisting me up. "What have you done?"

Smoke induced tears streamed from my reddened eyes. I scarcely recognized the voice, but judging by the lack of a brutal assault, this man knew me... at least a little. "What? Are you stupid?" The words spilled out reflexively, which was not the wisest thing.

The guard's grip tightened on my arm before he shoved me back. The man peered over at the lingering cloud of smoke and coughed. His brown eyes turned back to me, narrowing. "Judging by your current state, and the smell, I will give you the benefit of the doubt. Still, I'd mind your tongue, boy. Which way did that woman go?"

If he followed, or even if his men followed, they'd likely die. But was that my decision to make? "It sounded like she rode south. I could only hear; I couldn't see, and thanks to that damn gas, I can't smell anything."

The guard grunted in response, releasing me. "Get out of here."

"Captain, the men are ready. What do you want us to do next?"

"We go south."

I watched as the captain disappeared behind the wall, only to come riding through the gate a moment later. The sound of hysteria filled the night sky. People screamed as they continued to flee the castle. Guards shouted orders, horses shrieked as adrenaline coursed through them, and although I should have checked on Stasya, I knew I had to seek more help. Except, I knew the only place I'd get it was the last place to offer it. But I had to go back to headquarters, regardless.

Sabrina would laugh in my face.

———

UPON ARRIVING AT HEADQUARTERS, I stormed inside and found Lukas speaking to one of the newer recruits. He lifted his brow and inclined his head toward the stairs. Without hesitating, I ran up the flight and toward the main office, where Sabrina sat.

"The king is dead," I huffed out, winded after running for nearly an hour.

Her dark red eyebrows furrowed, then smoothed out. "That's too bad." Sabrina's lips pressed into a thin line as she surveyed my appearance; I was still dressed in a well-tailored suit, my slicked-back hair had taken on its mussed appearance again, and the skin beneath my eyes tightened. My knuckles whitened as I clenched my fists, and Sabrina *tsked* at me.

"Calm down, Nik," she said, maneuvering around the desk. "Take a breath—or five."

Unclenching my fists, I turned away from her and caught my reflection in a picture frame. My eyes flickered between their natural yellow to the phosphorescent shade they took on before I shifted. Young wolves shifted when their emotions flared to life, but in my life, I had never been accused of being emotional. I was angry, but why?

"I am calm," I supplied, rubbing my hand along the back of my neck. "If I wasn't, I wouldn't be here." Which was true. I would have been galloping down the woods, hunting that damn woman. Feathers would have littered the ground by now and her wings would be pinned to the castle walls for all to see.

Sabrina lifted her eyebrows and leaned against her desk, folding her arms. "I'll give you that. It's unfortunate King Ansgar is dead, but you know we cannot and will not offer our assistance in the matter. We don't—"

"Get involved in politics. I know, but I thought you'd want to know about another assassin running about. A woman no less. She walked into the royal ball as if she belonged there. Interestingly enough, she spoke like she belonged there, too." I turned my back to Sabrina, shifting my jaw. This was a mess, and all because I became distracted. I wanted to see Stasya. I selfishly wanted to spend time with her and tease her—*why?* I saw Stasya, looking the part of a moonlit queen, but it was what I felt, not what I saw that sparked a gnawing feeling inside of me. I felt the familiar tug of a bond longing to snap into place, and another foreign feeling that I suspected was jealousy. Nothing in me wanted to feel it—numbness was something I knew. Whatever it was, *it* did me no good. The king was dead and while no part of me mourned the loss, it could have been Stasya.

Sabrina pushed off from the desk, her fingers catching on a scrap of paper. "We don't meddle in political affairs, but I am curious who that woman is and what role the Hawk plays in this game. We won't intervene, but I won't kick you out of this organization for breaking code. You must not drag us into this, understand? Should this woman make things more personal..." Sabrina's voice trailed off, and I wondered if she was implying she'd step in then and bring the force of the Huntsmen down on the bird. "We won't acknowledge this; not unless it comes to our doorstep."

Silence filled the space between us. I focused on the steady thumping of my heart. The sound of each breath I took, and little by little I felt the tension ease from my body.

Sabrina folded the paper in her grasp and spun around on her heel. "Get some sleep." She waved her hand, dismissing me from her office. I wondered if that was an assignment she wanted to discuss, but her body language brooked no room for an argument, and I had no energy to debate. Without another word, I left the room.

Sleep called to me in the spare room upstairs, as did anything but this suit. My fingers nimbly unbuttoned the linen dress shirt, and rather than neatly pile everything in the chair by the dresser, I left a trail of clothes in my wake. By the time I made it to the bed, I was half asleep. When I closed my eyes, the last image I saw was the accusatory look in Stasya's eyes.

———

WHEN I WOKE up the next morning, I felt rather than saw a pair of eyes on me. I bolted upward, the blankets tumbling from my chest and pooling around my hips. "A knock would suffice," I drawled, pinning the figure with a cold, yellow-eyed stare.

Lukas folded the shirt I wore last night and placed it on the dresser as he stood to his feet. "It's my establishment. A knock is a courtesy—not a requirement." He paused and twisted his lips as if he was trying to figure out how to word his next statement. "Sabrina told me what happened. I don't blame you for this—"

"As if I would care if you did. But I'm glad you don't because it wasn't my doing. Ansgar made a deal with the feathered demoness long before I strolled onto the scene." Mentioning Ansgar caused my heart rate to spike. I loathed that man for many reasons. However, the one at the top of the list wasn't because of my mother—it was Stasya and Edda. Endangering his daughters for a petty reason was unforgivable. Locking Stasya up in a dungeon—as if she were only a common pet—that was condemnable, and the gods punished him justly.

As Lukas' hand left the folded shirt, he brought a fist to his chest and then relaxed it. I had a way of slicing through his collected disposition and settling beneath his skin to fester. "Are you still capable of working here while you deal with your personal life?" he asked.

Pursing my lips, I squinted my eyes as I looked at him, wondering what the hell he was getting at. My personal life? The kingdom's politics had little to do with my personal life, but something in my chest twisted and disagreed. Frustrated with the conflicted feeling, I raked my fingers along my scalp, snarling. "Of course. Isn't that why your sister wanted me here? Because of my ability–or lack thereof– when dealing with personal things?" I snapped at him and tossed the blankets off.

One minute Lukas was standing by the dresser and the next he was in front of me, his fist flying toward my face. I blocked it, using his momentum to pull him toward me. My knee was waiting for him, but Lukas was quick and knew how to dodge to the side to avoid my blow. Before my foot connected with him, he swept my other leg out from under me, and I crashed to the floor. His foot stomped beside my head just as I rolled to the side, which allowed for an opening to spring to my feet with an arm outstretched as if I had a blade. I jabbed my finger into Lukas' neck to signify I stabbed him in the jugular.

A chuckle escaped Lukas, and he grinned. "For a butcher, you're skilled, but for an assassin, you need improvement." His finger grazed my bare rib. "You'd be dead, too. You need more training on your groundwork, Nik. You're fast, and you're strong, but if you lack technique, what is the point?"

"I don't care," I said.

"Let me rephrase that, you don't have a choice—you have to train."

"No, I mean, I don't care that I'd be dead." Pausing for a moment, I added, "But, if it'll stop your nagging, I'll suffer your training sessions."

Lukas' brows furrowed, my words taking him by surprise. It was unnatural perhaps, to not have that want to survive. I didn't want to die, and to take my life had never crossed my mind, but the thought of dying didn't send me into a panic. I suppose the idea of Liesel being alone had always driven me onward. What if I was gone—who would tell her the stories Ma used to? If I was gone, who would keep those memories alive?

"I care, kid. I care." Lukas dropped his hand and backed off. It was the first time he had ever expressed something outside of annoyance with me. I kept my mouth shut and waited for him to explain why he was in my room while I only wore my freckles.

"Your next assignment... it's interesting." He lowered his gaze and pulled a paper from his pocket. It was worn and beaten like the one I saw Sabrina holding yesterday. "We didn't take money for this, so understand that you won't receive payment."

My brows dipped down, and a frown curved my lips. The Seidel's weren't a generous family—nevermind leaders of an assassins league—which made me wonder why they took on this job for free.

"There is a boy in Bromiel, whose father bea—"

Lukas didn't need to utter another word. All I needed to know was that a kid needed to escape a hellish life. "I'll take it." I snatched the paper from him and glanced down at it. The chicken scratch that stared up at me wasn't directed toward the Huntsmen—it was to someone—anyone. A desperate cry for help from a miserable existence. An abusive, drunken father, a life of misery and hunt. Signed by a kid named Frederik.

"Sabrina found the letter on one of her assignments. She did a little investigating after and found out where he lives. He's around your age, give or take a year." Turning to the dresser, Lukas pulled out a pair of pants and a shirt, tossed it at me, and motioned with his hand to dress.

"Why?" I yanked my shirt down and slid into my pants,

knotting them in place. "Why help someone like him, and for free?"

A dark look passed over Lukas' face, his jaw muscles leaping. "We didn't have a kind father, and I swore to protect my sister. So I did, but I failed to protect our mother." Running a hand along his face, Lukas walked toward the bedroom door. "Imagine being alone with no one to protect you, let alone help you." He sighed, then added, "We are not angels, but I'd like to think sometimes we're cleansing this world of filth."

Lukas left me alone with my thoughts, which centered on being eradicators of refuse. The state of my soul meant little to me, and the red that stained my hands didn't keep me up at night, but what Lukas had said pricked me. Imagining someone like my sister—or even a younger Lukas—suffering at the hands of someone like this Frederik's father—or even my father. I'd do this assignment twenty times over if I had to. It would also allow me time to gather resources on the Hawk.

Bromiel would take only an hour to get there, which meant before I left, I would have to drag Raif into my scheming. Raif didn't know it, but he was going on an assignment soon.

———

OUTSIDE OF HEADQUARTERS, Raif held a sword he crafted a few days ago—a longer blade with a crossguard I had never seen before. One piece of metal curved upward and another down, so that no matter if the blade was upward or downward it would catch the opponent's weapon. It was different, but I never laughed at Raif's ideas or his unique weapons. He knew what he was doing.

Sheathing the blade, he turned to face me and promptly signed, *"No."*

A grin formed on my face. His fingers met with enough gusto that they snapped, and I imagined his word rumbling in my head. "You don't even know what I'm going to ask."

Shifting the blade's scabbard under his arm, Raif signed. *"I don't need to. I'll say no to your scheming every time."*

"I can't be in two places at once, and I need your help."

"I'm not doing your assignment for you."

"Which is fine, because I'm not asking you to. This is about Sta—"

Raif's nose wrinkled, his hazel-green eyes igniting before his hands made quick work of his words—they were fast, and furious. *"I will not be the undoing of that poor girl's life. I followed you once into that mess and it was a mistake."* His dark brows furrowed as he glowered at me.

"Undoing... I gave her a taste of freedom, and I'll admit, my judgment was clouded on that part." It always seemed to be around her, but in Raif's defense, he was right. She could have died in the forest, just outside of the castle walls. I wanted her to taste freedom, and the Hawk wanted payment.

"You used her to lure out the Hawk, and she almost died. You almost died."

"But I didn't." I ran my hand along my face, frustrated with Raif and myself. "I just want you to make sure she stays safe, that's all. You need not do anything but keep your eyes and ears open."

I never groveled but I so desperately wanted Stasya to be

safe. I also didn't trust that foreign prince, either. "Please," I said, nearly cringing. The word felt foreign, but more than that it was the emotion behind the word or rather the desperation.

Raif's eyes widened. He knew me well enough now to know the word please never passed my lips. *"Is she..."* His fingers signed and then, *"She's your other half?"* A breath escaped his nose, his lips pulled back to reveal a flash of white teeth.

Yes. I wanted to snarl the reply. It didn't matter—what mattered was that she stayed safe—if that meant I stayed away from her and watch as Prince Ass-Roy swept her away, then so be it. But I'd be lying if I said it wasn't a maddening feeling.

There were stories about wolves who had bonded and were driven apart, forced to live their lives with others and it drove them mad. It ground against their mental state and physical. I was born twisted, so who could say how much of that I could endure, but I had one thing going for me and it was that I wasn't bonded to Stasya—not yet. I felt the call tug me closer, but if I ignored it, ran from it, maybe we could escape that fate.

"It doesn't matter."

"I'll do it."

A tense breath escaped my lungs, sounding more like a groan of relief. I nodded my thanks to Raif. Now, it was time to figure out how to get Raif inside when I couldn't be. I knew now more than ever if they caught me in the castle I'd be killed without question. I doubted Stasya would order me killed, but the guards would no doubt enjoy taking the killing blow.

Raif, however, was a shadow they didn't know. He also had a kinder way of dealing with people than I did. Maybe he could win some points with the staff.

"This time I have a say in how things go down or I won't do it. Mate or not, Nik."

I could live with that, and before I left for Bromiel, we'd have a plan and I'd have a way into the castle, a way to keep an eye on Stasya and know that she was safe.

CHAPTER 2

A FEW DAYS LATER, Raif and I met up. "You did what?" I asked, gawking at Raif. A smug smile split his lips wide and his pearly white teeth gleamed in the afternoon sun. Bastard.

"Fortune favors the bold." Raif signed with his hands.

Fortune, so it seemed, loathed me and perhaps it sensed that something tainted me to the core. Who could say? But fortune worked in Raif's favor, which was fine because it allowed for us to pounce on opportunity.

"Let me get this straight, you waltzed into the castle and demanded the position of a blacksmith?" Jamming my fingers into my hair, I stared at him incredulously.

"I don't waltz *anywhere."* His brows knit together, then he laughed soundlessly, shoulders shaking. *"I heard a rumor that there was a position opening for an apprentice. It pays better than the village, and I showed him my wares. They thought my craft was on par with their current master, so there you have it. I am now an apprentice in the castle."*

A week, that was how long it had been since I asked Raif to help. A week since I began planning my trip to Bromiel to deal with that kid's father. How had it only been a week since my run-in with the Hawk?

Crossing my arms, I shook my head. "If I believed in any of the gods, I'd swear one has blessed you."

Raif turned his hazel-green eyes on me and shook his head vehemently. *"They owe me."*

Didn't the gods all owe us something? Always testing their subjects. Always taking things away, harming those who least deserve it, while others climbed their way to a life of luxury when they should have lain in a bed of filth.

"They owe us all."

———

WHILE I PACKED for the trip to Bromiel, I thought of how I would have handled my father differently if given the chance to again. I was angry and irrational when I killed him. It was easy—almost too easy—like half the fight in him had left already. Maybe it did—his mate was dead—did he care? Did it drive him mad to feel that tether snap? My mouth opened, jaw shifting before it clenched shut. I know I didn't care that my father was dead, and to give him any thought other than pummeling into the dirt again was dishonoring my mother.

If I could kill him again, how would I do it? It was a dark thought, but the way he treated Ma deserved a lifetime of punishment—not just a few moments.

Cinching the pack closed, I turned around just when Sabrina rapped her fingers on the door to the guest room. "I'd ask how you are feeling after an intense week of training with Lukas, but..."

Training with Lukas was always excruciating. He enjoyed tormenting me and I made him pay for it—he may have known more techniques, but he couldn't argue with the strength behind my hits as they connected with him. This week, Lukas endured every hard hit, every snarky remark and said nothing as he gingerly walked away. That surprised me, yet the upcoming trip to Bromiel occupied my mind, and Stasya. I had little room for thoughts of Lukas.

"Tell Lukas to use comfrey leaves and boil them down before applying it to the deep bruises." Shouldering the bag, I walked out of the room, pushing past Sabrina. Her eyes widened. Perhaps she forgot that my mother was a healer, but I didn't, and I kept some of her knowledge.

Sabrina made an audible noise with her tongue. "You and I will have yet another chat when you return—this pertains to Raif." Her intelligent green eyes fixed on me, and no part of her face said it amused her. Amusement curled my lips up into a devilish grin.

If I could live a dual life, it couldn't have been that complicated for another person. Shrugging, I nodded my head in Sabrina's direction. "I expect a thorough interrogation when I return." I turned my head to the side, chuckling as I winked at her.

———

OUTSIDE OF HEADQUARTERS, I stood on the edge of the woods. I had two options, shift and risk being hunted, or ride a horse into the bleak town and stick out like a sore thumb. Bromiel was poor, with little foot traffic into the main part of the village. If I rode in, it would already cause the villagers to take notice, whereas if I snuck in and blended in with the villagers, they'd think nothing of my being there.

Deciding against riding, I methodically removed my clothing and packed it away. All I needed to do was think about my other form, and my body did the rest. In one moment, I stood as a man, and in the next, I was a beast covered in red fur. Bending my head down, I gripped the pack and darted into the cover of the woods.

An hour into the journey, the sun lost its battle with the canopy of trees. Tall pines blocked whatever warmth the winter sun would have provided. More than that, it blocked the smoke from escaping the immediate area. It tickled my nose and burned my eyes. I took the opportunity to shift safely, then dress.

This was my destination. Bromiel in all its gloomy, dismal glory. Some said wraiths lurked in the wood, that they were the ones responsible for shrouding the village. I didn't believe it, but it was a strange thing to walk into the village in the middle of a sunny day and find as little sun in the sky as what one did during dusk.

A gentle breeze whispered across the back of my neck, it felt refreshing against my warm flesh. Winter had crept into the lands, and the scent of decomposing leaves tickled my nose. It was sweet from the leaves mixing with the acidic needles of the fir trees around.

Sabrina said this kid lived across from a tanner, which meant I could rely on my nose to point me in the right direction. I just had to follow the scent of death, and dyes.

Past the smell of burning wood and cooking food, I caught the trail of death laced with oak remnants. That was no doubt the tanner's shop which would leave me at the doorstep of Frederik.

In front of the tanner's, a wolf pelt hung stretched. The eyeless sockets stared up at the sky, mouth open in a soundless cry. A pit formed in my stomach, not out of nerves but anger. It was a common wolf—not a werewolf—yet knowing there were those that prided themselves in hunting were-wolves, killing them for their large pelts or only because they were different still gnawed at me.

I heard rather than saw someone milling around outside near the back of a wooden hut. The wood they built the house with was barely a step up from sticks, and the thatched roof looked as if it were about to cave in. Sidestepping, I edged forward and clung to the shadows of the hut.

"Stupid, stupid. Why did you do that? Just keep your mouth shut, Freddy. That's it. You should know better," the voice repeated fretfully.

Creeping up on the individual, I spotted a slender redhead. His skin made my paleness look tan, but instead of being a shock of red, his head was a rich shade of auburn. The boy was bent over a dead chicken, feathers strewn about as he angrily plucked them. Blood coated his hands, and the head lay near his feet. It wasn't a clean butchering in the least.

"Stupid, stupid," he repeated. Stiffening a moment later, his head cocked to the side, and when he turned, I could see a stream of tears. Red rimmed his alarmingly green eyes. "Who are you?" he demanded, his hand snatching up the cleaver on the chopping block near him.

"I know what you are, and who you are." The scent of him wafted toward me, mingling with the dead chicken. He was a wolf, too.

The sniffling boy used his hand to wipe away the tears, smearing downy feathers and blood across his cheek. "You shouldn't be here. He'll find you, find us, and he'll hurt you," he whispered.

Maybe not, but here I was. No one would hurt Frederik.

Stepping closer, I noted how frail and little he was. He couldn't have been much younger than me. Maybe two years? Yet he looked as though he had been crafted of porcelain. His face was open, tortured, and he looked so young and helpless. "But I am." Shrugging, I edged closer and eyed the knife in his grasp. "You're Frederik, right?"

Frederik whirled around, his eyes narrowing and full lips pressing into a thin line. "How do you know my name? I don't know you." His eyes searched me frantically, and he waved the knife around. "Why are you here?"

Arching a brow, I lifted my hands to show I meant no harm to him. "You wrote a letter, remember? Asking for help. I'm here to help." A wild look entered his eyes—desperation, glee, and fear.

"No, I don't believe you," he whispered. "You're here because of him, aren't you? He sent you to punish me?" Frederik dropped the chicken onto the chopping block and blindly glanced around. "I wasn't bad, I was stupid, but I wasn't bad."

I didn't know what he was rambling about, but I knew what his body language said. It said he was desperate; he felt cornered, and he was about to lash out. "Frederik, put down the cleaver. I will only ask once. I'm here to help you." Scared or not, I wasn't keen on him having a weapon at his disposal.

The boy's lips twisted, and his dark brows narrowed before he launched at me. Weapon held high, readying to sweep down at my neck, except there was no grace to the boy's movements. I twisted his arm, disarming him, and used his momentum to send him hurtling to the ground. He landed with a thud and promptly scrambled into a crouch. I used my foot and shoved him onto his back, pushing down with slight pressure. "Don't. I am not here for you. You wanted your father gone. I don't want to hurt you. I can take care of him, if that's what you want."

Frederik's eyes widened, his face flushed, and his mouth gaped open. "What?" His voice cracked as he stared up at me.

"It's your choice."

His shoulders fell forward as tension fled his body, Frederik's green eyes darted to the side. "G-gone for good? You'd do that?"

"You can't get much gone-r than dead." A grin tugged at my lips as I released my hold on him. If someone had given me the chance years ago, I would have leaped at it. I would have beaten my old man into the ground years ago.

"Can... Can I tell you how to do it?" He licked his lips and sat up slowly. "No, no, Freddy," he mumbled and grinned wildly at the dead chicken. "I want to do it."

Whatever I expected, it wasn't that. This wasn't the typical hit, and Frederik wasn't exactly all there. One look at the kid and it was easy to see, but listening to him was another matter, too. "Frederik, I don't think..."

"He's asleep right now. Passed out from late night drinking," he rambled. "We could go inside, and he'd never know." A laugh escaped him. His hand slapped over his mouth quickly but his shoulders continued to quake.

Narrowing my eyes on him, I folded my arms and watched. "Does he hit you?"

"Hit me?" Frederik breathed the words and hurriedly pulled at his shirt. I held my hands out to stop him, but he continued to yank on his shirt until the fabric pulled away and fell to the ground. Ugly bruises covered his porcelain skin, but the silver, raised flesh on his back caught my eye. Not just one raised scar, but several, and different shapes. Frederik had endured more than he ever ought to by the hands of his father.

"All right." A part of me knew I should just go inside, quickly use my dagger and finish. Yet, I knew on some level what this kid had gone through. "All right," I repeated. "I will help you."

CHAPTER 3

So I helped him. As we crept inside the hut, it was silent aside from the occasional crackle from the hearth. Moving around a makeshift divider, I saw a man on a lone cot. I didn't have to ask Frederik where his bed was because I had seen the rumpled blankets on the dirt floor.

Stepping toward the cot, I stood over Frederik's father, watching as he snored away. How easy it would have been to snuff the life from him right then, but the shaky breathing behind me reminded me that this was not my decision. Bending down, I pulled on his arms, beginning to secure his wrist to the bed. So heavily inebriated, he only woke when I tightened the rope on his other wrist.

"Who are you? What are you doing in my house?" he slurred. "Frederik, where the hell are you?" Spittle flecked the man's mouth and a wild look entered his gaze as he thrashed.

My eyes narrowed as I finished tying his legs down to his cot. I tore a fraction of his sheet and balled it up in my palm. "I am no one. Don't worry, Frederik is right here." Looking over my shoulder, I wanted to give the kid one last chance to back out, to let me handle this, but when I saw the resolve in his eyes, and the way he stalked forward, I knew he made up his mind. "I'll be outside." I shoved the fabric in the man's mouth before stalking outside. Perhaps it was wicked, but it was justice to me. *Wicked justice* had a ring to it in my mind.

Once the kid finished, he came outside covered in blood and a smile on his face. Some may call me possessed, but when I killed, I felt nothing. No sadness, no glee, but when I looked at Frederik, I saw joy or at the very least, satisfaction.

"He is dead," Frederik said with a smile.

"Good." I nodded.

"Thank you." Frederik blinked. Blood dripped from his brow and onto his cheek. "For freedom, for retribution."

I did no such thing. This kid couldn't stay here, and he was homeless now. While his tormentor was dead, so was the comfort of a home, whatever comfort he had there.

"You can't stay here. Look, take this and go. I don't know where, but you can't be here when the rest of the village wakes. Go." Reaching into my pocket, I pulled out a pouch full of coin and handed it to him. It was enough that he could feed himself and find housing if he didn't spend it foolishly. "Just run, Frederik. You'll survive, but if you stay, they will hunt you down here—even if he deserved it—you know that. For the sake of everyone, find a place to wash the blood off, and grab those clothes I saw hanging up."

A wild look entered his eyes, but Frederik nodded. "What about you?" he asked, taking the coin pouch. "Where will you go?" He sounded like a lost little boy.

Cocking my head, I glanced over at him. It would do no one any good if he knew where I truly went, or that this was a normal occurrence for me. "I'll be fine. Take care of yourself." Frederik darted for his clothes, then ran into the woods.

I waited for a moment before I stepped into the woods and shifted.

Shaking off an eerie feeling, I ran as fast as I could to headquarters.

———

When I reached headquarters, I was out of breath and near exhaustion. The past week had sucked the life out of me. Strategically stepping behind one of our training targets, I pulled on my clothes and glanced up at the balcony to see Sabrina staring down at me. She was furious. I could tell by the way her lips pressed together and how she stood rigid.

"We have a problem," she ground out. "Get in here."

Leave it to me to find trouble when I wasn't even there to do the digging. Dragging myself inside, I glanced around and discovered no one was lingering around. No laughs rang out, no sound of training.

Lukas approached me, handing me a letter. "That was quick," he said. His eyes ran over me, likely trying to gauge if I was wounded or not.

"Quick and odd. I'll fill you in on it after," I said between sucking in a breath. Almost immediately my brows furrowed. A glob of green wax sealed the paper, but it was the emblem inside that had me looking to Sabrina. The royal seal of Abendrot depicted a wolf swiping at an unseen enemy, and around it the words said, "We fall together and we rise together."

Sabrina bellowed for me upstairs, prolonging the opening of the royal letter. Sighing, I made my way upstairs and to the office, where I found Sabrina covered in blood. It stained her shirt, her hands and face.

"What the hell happened?" Exhaustion fled and replacing it was curiosity then fury. "Are you okay?"

"It isn't mine." She wrung her hands and motioned toward the next room. "It's Breck's, and he's dead."

It took a moment for my mind to register her words. Breck, who had always been a friend of the Seidel's. Breck, who built his fair share of Walddorf's homes. "Why? How?"

Sabrina pulled up a tattered piece of paper and another item that caused a snarl to tear free. A feather. A crisp, clean feather. "He was dead when we found him on the training grounds. He had this note and feather on his body."

Dearest Huntsmen,

I hope this letter finds you well. Apologies for the body. Sometimes, to get one's attention, we must spill blood. I'm glad you're listening now because I want you to know, Abendrot will be mine, and I'll enjoy watching it crumble from the inside out.

A weak ruler can never hope to rule a weak kingdom. It's nothing personal, but please keep your ill-trained, and filthy hands off my men.

Yours truly,
The Hawk

EVERY MUSCLE in my body tensed. The hand which had the

note in it tightened, crumpling the piece of paper. "I never meant—" I never meant for this to fall on the Huntsmen. I never wanted them to become involved as a whole, but now the Hawk didn't just drag them into it. She shoved their faces in it.

"No. You didn't do this. Eventually, she would have come knocking if it's the kingdom she wants." She pinched the bridge of her nose then let her hand fall by her side. "I've changed my mind. The Huntsmen will partake in this hunt for that feathered wretch. It's now personal."

Relief—or something close to it—allowed me to relax. Exhaling, I lifted the letter with the royal seal and quickly read it.

NIKLAUS,

Come to the castle at once. Use the main gates, as you'll find the castle heavily guarded, and they have been given strict instructions to kill first and ask questions later.

-Stasya

LIFTING my eyes from the letter, my hands tore the parchment into miniscule pieces. Did the Hawk already infiltrate the castle? Had they learned something? "I need to go."

Sabrina stopped in her tracks. "Do you need one of our horses?"

"No. As much as my body would prefer that, I don't think it's the fastest." The horse couldn't travel in a straight line, it had to stick to trails, highways, and paths that were beaten down, but wolves? We could run through briars, we could go where horses could not. Exhaustion weighed on me, forming circles beneath my eyes and creating aches all over my body. I was tired from traveling, but exhaustion was my constant companion, so it would seem.

Nodding her head, Sabrina stepped forward and took the bag from my shoulder. "Come with me." I followed her down the hallway stairs and to the front hall. "Take your clothes off and hand them to me." Pointing toward the empty study over her shoulder, she motioned for me to get inside.

I did as she instructed, and peeled off the layers of clothing, carefully taking out the weapons that were hidden in various pockets. Sabrina placed those inside the bag. Once I was as bare as a newborn, I let myself shift comfortably. It was a fluid shift as I gave myself over to the beast within.

Sabrina turned around, lifted her brows and a small gasp came from her. "Oh." Stepping forward, she closed the distance between us. "I've never seen one of you up close."

Likely for the best, considering most of the humans were out to kill us—little did they know we surrounded them.

"Sorry to say this, Nik, you're kind of beautiful." She reached out and scratched at a tuft of fur behind my ear. I emitted a low rumble in protest, but she laughed and did it again.

As I stepped out of the study, she shrunk back and regarded me with fascination. In this form, I was tall for our kind, just as I was as human. The top of my head reached her chest, which made me quite the formidable foe.

"Here," she said, looping the bag around my neck so I could change into clothes later. "Don't get killed; we'd hate to lose you." She ran a hand along my head, which was strange since she'd never touch me so personally before.

Sabrina pushed the door open and stood back. Regarding her with bright yellow eyes, I nodded my head and leaped out of the cottage, racing toward the deep woods that would take me to the castle.

———

THROUGH THE BRIARS, under fallen trees and between narrow pathways, I cut through the woods in a straight line which brought me to a clearing close to the royal forest. Panting heavily, I circled to gather my wits and allowed for my body to shift. Adrenaline coursed through my veins, fighting off the exhaustion that threatened to creep in.

Once dressed, I walked up the wood line toward the castle. I could see the spire, and the dark stone structure jutting out against the cloudy winter sky.

As I approached the road that led to the castle, every muscle in my body tensed; it felt like I was preparing for a war, and maybe I was. I knew the guards would prefer to slay me and throw me into a pile of rubble. However, I wasn't here for them; I was here for Stasya.

The iron gates towered over me, twisting and reaching toward the sky in a way that was to deter anyone from climbing it, lest they become impaled.

One guard turned and noted who I was. I remembered his face. He was one of the guards who carried me to the infirmary.

"You!" he barked out, reaching for his sword. "I should cut you down now."

Narrowing my eyes, I held up my hands. "You won't though." I was still fairly winded, and it'd take me a moment to recover. Pointing a finger toward the castle, I leaned forward slightly. "I'm here on official business." I winked. The guard was not as amused as I thought he'd be, instead he scowled and lifted his sword from his side. I remained calm, hands in the air. "Her Highness—Princess Stasya—asked for me."

Another guard approached. He wore a dark red sash at his waist, a stark contrast to the dark green leathers, and it told me he was the Captain of the Guard. "At ease. The princess is waiting for him." His subordinate sheathed the sword without a word, and moved to the side of the gate, using the crank to open it.

The Captain moved his hand from his blade and pulled manacles from his side. "The only way you're getting inside is if you're restrained." Securing them on my wrists, he smirked. "Follow me."

"Keep your fantasies to yourself, Captain."

Every muscle in the guard's body tensed, his eyes tightened, and jaw clenched. The Captain made it easy to crawl beneath his skin, but if he was an honorable sort—which I assumed he was—I was everything he loathed. I might as well have been the one to deal the killing blow to King Ansgar.

His elbow met my ribs roughly, causing me to wheeze and yet I couldn't help but chuckle as we walked into the castle.

CHAPTER 4

GUARDS MILLED AROUND, switching posts. Everywhere my eyes darted there was someone on duty, and it pleased me on some level that they took the security of the castle more seriously. I shouldn't have been able to slip in with such ease or whisk Stasya away into the woods like I did before this mess occurred.. I shouldn't have been able to sneak into the party, and yet I did.

The air inside the castle was damp and crisp—not so different from the winter air outside—but it lacked the scent of pine. Instead, it smelled of smoke and cooking herbs.

"Where is my fanfare?" I questioned, turning to the guard who was half a head shorter than me. He said nothing. "No feast in my honor then," I muttered petulantly.

"What do you know of honor? You're a murderer." He turned to a female servant. "Announce the Wolf, Her Highness awaits." The servant stole a glance, her tanned skinned paling considerably, then she vanished through the labyrinth of halls to wherever Stasya hid away.

I shifted my hands which made the guard slip his sword from his scabbard a fraction. Lifting my eyebrows, I opened my palms up to show him I had nothing and meant no harm. "Even murderers have a code they follow." I paused for a moment, thinking about what I said, then added, "At least the paid ones. The ones who get off on killing people—those sort have no honor."

Captain Honorable looked at me, his lip curling in disgust. "I don't know if I should pity you or..." His words cut off, then his attention pulled away from me, drawn toward the figure at the top of the stairs.

It wasn't Stasya. Instead, it was Prince Ashroy of Ishkertov. His pale hair nearly blended in with his skin, and those unearthly crystal blue eyes pinned me where I stood.

A snort escaped me, which gained an elbow to the stomach. I grunted and inclined my head. "Prince Assroy, is it?" I asked nonchalantly. The remark earned me a prompt kick to the back of my knees, sending me to the floor. I kneeled, chuckling.

"What a clever mind you have to come up with that all on your own." Ashroy descended the stairs, a pleasant but tight smile on his face. "Did you rehearse it?"

"Clever minds need not rehearse lines," I retorted. The captain snarled beside me but didn't say a word. If he thought kicking me to the floor would humble me, he thought wrong. I *allowed* for them to cuff me, bring me inside, and shove me to the floor. I allowed all of this. In a blink, I could have him on the ground gasping for breath— and with the prince at ease, I could likely get to him, too.

Folding his arms, Ashroy pressed his lips into a thin line. "Quite right, Niklaus. I applaud your efforts to stop the Hawk, but I don't understand why Stasya brought you here. You failed her—" His mouth snapped shut at the sound of voices approaching.

Stasya rounded the corner, her bright green eyes focusing on Ashroy, and then me. Calmness smoothed her features, but I knew better than to assume she was calm. I could smell her anxiety and fear, which sparked an odd sensation in me.

"Let him stand," Stasya ordered as she approached. Standing next to Ashroy, her eyes quickly appraised my well-being.

I wiggled my fingers in the cuffs as I stood to my feet. "And let him free."

"No. Those can remain in place." She nodded her head, then turned on her heel and walked down the nearby hall. "Let's speak in private." Flicking her hand, she motioned for the guard to escort me along.

Stasya led us down the hall, then into a small study. Bookshelves lined the walls, and it was so musty smelling that it threatened to make me sneeze. She approached a desk in the room's corner and picked up a piece of paper. "We received this two days ago." She glanced to Ashroy then to me.

My handler relinquished his grip on my elbow, allowing me the freedom to move toward Stasya. The smell of her washed over me, invading all of my senses. Strangely, I missed the way she would scold me, and how fear scarcely lit her green eyes. Lifting both of my hands, I took the paper from her and read it quickly.

The Hawk still wanted payment for breach of contract. She was coming for the rest of the royal family—whatever was left of it. "You had nothing to do with it."

"Be that as it may, someone has to clean up my father's many messes." A twinge of sadness crept into her tone. "He was an imperfect ruler, with many regrets in the end."

Now was not the time to gripe about King Ansgar or to

bring up my ever-growing list of how despicable he was. When it came down to it, I likely would have been the one to deal the killing blow sooner rather than later, but someone beat me to it.

"The Hawk means to take the kingdom, but before she does that, she wants to watch it crumble." What had Ansgar been thinking? How could he have been so blind and so foolish?

"What? How do you know this?" Stasya gasped and motioned to the guard.

"Because, before arriving here, she sent a rather loud message." The guard made his way toward me and unlocked the manacles. I dropped one hand but held onto the paper with the other. "What do you want me here for, Stasya?" Because I knew she wanted something from me, and it wasn't just to see me cuffed.

Casting her eyes downward, she visibly warred with what she was about to say. "I need your help. Abendrot is on the brink of crumbling, and if what you say is true... The Hawk is waiting for it. The debt my father incurred whilst ruling is outrageous, and he made several enemies." She paused and bridged the gap between us, but not before sharing a look with Ashroy. "I'm afraid for Edda."

Edda, whose cherubic face reminded me so much of my little sister. Edda who was the fire to her sister's ice. "Fine. I'll help you."

Stasya looked puzzled, her brows furrowing, but the expression softened into warmth—relaxation even. "You don't even know what I would ask of you."

"If it is protecting either you or Edda, I'll do it." I handed her the paper and turned to look at Ashroy. "What are *you* going to do?" I wondered if his father knew of how dire the situation was here...if he knew how quickly the country was crumbling and if that was why his son was ushered in so conveniently. "What are you doing here?"

"Niklaus," Stasya snapped.

I would not listen. My eyes latched onto Ashroy's and I walked forward. "Well? Where is *your* clever remark, or are you too busy rehearsing it?"

Ashroy's long fingers swept along his lips, attempting to smooth out a smile. "I need not answer to you, Niklaus. I am here for Stasya and Edda. I *was* here for them."

I laughed and bared my teeth, nose wrinkling before slamming my palms into the prince's chest. "So you are, princeling, but what are you going to do when the Hawk comes for one of them like a thief in the night?" I rammed my palms into his chest again, this time with more force so he stumbled backward. To Ashroy's credit, he didn't rouse, but the guard did. Immediately, I lifted my hands up and backed away.

"Niklaus!" Stasya pulled at my shirt and inserted herself between us. "Enough of this. Ashroy and I have discussed this at length."

"Of course you have," I snapped at her. Her hand struck my face in a blur, leaving a reddened welt behind. Every muscle in my body grew rigid. A rumbling growl escaped me, which set everyone in the room on edge.

"Stop this at once. You are not here for Ashroy or to bait one another. You are here to *help us*. Please, if not for me, then at least for Edda."

I didn't want to be this close to either of them. The scent of Stasya seemed to muddle my senses more and more it seemed, and if I stood next to Ashroy, I would punch him in his pretty face. "I said I will—I meant it." Now that I was back from my mission, I could fully commit to hunting the Hawk. The issue wasn't hunting her, the issue was being in two places at once. "I can offer help, but your guards may not like it."

"Enlighten us," Ashroy demanded.

"One of my own. He recently took a position here as the blacksmith's apprentice." Ignoring the looks, I ran a hand down my face. "And I can offer more. The Huntsmen will go to war with this winged devil. Raif is already here. I trust him with my life, and so I'll trust him with yours." That was the truth. Raif was solid, trustworthy, and when it came to wielding a weapon, he was an unstoppable force.

Stasya averted her gaze and nodded to Ashroy. "Leave us for a moment. You are dismissed, Alric." When the guard hesitated, she waved her hand. "If he meant to harm me—which he doesn't—he would have done so months ago. Leave us, Captain." Her voice hardened, and once the two exited the room, she shut the door.

Energy crackled in the room. I felt it, tasted it, and because of that, I folded my arms, not entirely trusting myself. "Does he know what you are?"

"No. It will remain that way, as it isn't your secret to share." Stasya crossed the room and sat on the edge of the wooden table in the room. Her eyes locked onto mine and in that instant, I saw her pupils dilate. "I will tell him when the time is right, which isn't now."

Unfolding my arms, I strode forward and planted my hands on either side of Stasya. I moved my head closer; we shared one another's breath, and it surprised me when she didn't move away. "I wouldn't tell him. That is your choice, Stasya." What I wanted was for her to be safe, also, I wanted her to be happy. It was a maddening feeling, one that I wish I could scrape from my being, yet I couldn't.

"You and your choices," she muttered, lifting a hand to press against my chest. It held no force behind it, so I didn't budge.

"Life is full of them. No one should strip your choices away or your freedom," I offered pointedly.

She snorted, causing my lips to turn into a devilish grin. My mouth parted with the start of a clever remark, but before I had a chance, her lips were on mine. It wasn't a tentative kiss; it was rushed and heated. The hand Stasya held against my chest slid to the back of my neck and I was all too eager to oblige her as I moved between her legs.

Cupping her cheek, I tilted her head back so I could deepen the kiss, allowing my tongue to brush against hers. Every inch she gave, I took it greedily, but never more than that.

She moved back, and I followed her, all but laying on top of her as our lips and tongues collided. A soft moan escaped her which encouraged me to move my hands up her thighs and to her hips.

When she pulled away, her green eyes blazed with a mixture of emotions I couldn't read. "I hate you," she whispered, but didn't retract herself from me. Her hand lifted to my cheek and her thumb brushed along the smattering of freckles.

It was easier to hate me, I supposed, than to allow herself to feel anything more. My eyes closed for a moment, enjoying the gentle touch from her. I turned my head, placing feather-light kisses to the inside of her arm.

"Justice finds a way. I believe that, but my father didn't have to die." Stasya's bottom lip quivered as she spoke, and I hated it. She deserved to cry—to mourn the loss of her father —but to see her reduced to tears disquieted something in me. Did she blame me for his death? She could, if it made her feel better.

"Stasya." More words tumbled in my mind, but I didn't say another word. I slid onto the table and she pressed her head against my chest. I wrapped my arms around her, letting her cry for her father. There were no words to comfort her, because it wasn't all right. All I could do was offer a reprieve from the farce she put on for the country.

I pulled her into my lap and stroked her back which seemed to pull her out of her sorrow. She moved her head away, wiped the tears from her eyes and built up the wall around her emotions. "I will do whatever it takes to keep my sister safe, and my country, Niklaus." One of my eyebrows arched in question before she continued. "If it means building an alliance with Ishkertov, then I will." She slid from my lap, wiping the tears away furiously.

A moment ago, she had her lips against mine and she dared to throw Ashroy into the conversation? I stood to my feet and ran a hand down my face to smooth out whatever harsh lines that were beginning to form. "Because of your father's prior decision or your own?" Confusion and frustration plastered itself on my face.

Her pale, fine brows knit together. "My own," she paused and folded her arms across her chest, as if feeling vulnerable. "This couldn't last—me and you. I am to be crowned queen at the end of the season and the country needs strength. They need a united team of rulers. Ashroy is—"

"A pretentious *arschgeige*," I continued. My teeth clamped down as a curse escaped me. If that was Stasya's decision, I respected it, but boundaries were coming, and she would not cross them again. "Fine."

"Fine? That's it?" Her eyes widened in surprise.

Narrowing my eyes, I planted a hand on my hip, cocking a leg. "Would you like me to throw a gauntlet down to fight for your hand? I won't. This isn't a game. You've made your decision and I'll respect it, but respect mine when I say this will no longer happen." I motioned to us, to the table. "Raif will take my place. Anything you need, you can ask him, and I'll hunt the Hawk down. Once the threat is eradicated, we will go on with our lives—you as queen, and me as the *Big Bad Wolf*. But mark my words, Stasya. I will not be your plaything. Not now, and not ever."

Stasya shifted her jaw but didn't look at me. "And one more thing..." Drumming my fingers in annoyance on the doorframe, I growled my next words. "Make sure there is someone that knows how to sign around. Raif will need it." I used it as my cue to exit the room and wasn't surprised to see Captain 'Honorable' Alric, or Ashroy looming near the door. Scowling, I showed myself the way out.

CHAPTER 5

A DAY—THAT was what I gave myself before I ventured to Raif's home. I needed a day to collect my wits, to shake the feeling of Stasya against me. It was a good thing I gave myself a day to calm down, because Kina, Raif's twin sister, emerged from their home with a sword in hand, leveled at my heart.

Rolling my eyes, I raised my hands and sighed. "Not today. Is Raif home?" It was early morning, and I guessed Raif was home.

The sword didn't budge, Kina jabbed it forward but didn't connect with me. "No. He isn't. I don't know what you got him involved in..."

I squinted, looking over her shoulder as Raif appeared in the doorway. "Don't look now, Kina, it's not-home-Raif," I said tersely.

Raif's hands raised to pull his unruly sandy curls from his face and he tied them back. With his hands free, he signed. "*What is it?*"

My gaze flicked to Kina and then back to Raif. "Aside from your sister's threats on my life? A proposition."

"No more propositions from you!" Kina hissed, lifting her blade and twisting it so that the flat of it would strike me. It didn't have time to—I caught the hilt in my grasp and kicked her legs out from under her so she fell to the ground in a heap. Raif didn't move. He glared at me, but he didn't move, likely because he knew it could have been worse.

Twisting the sword in the air, I planted the tip into the ground and leaned on the pommel. "As I was saying, I need to speak to Raif. Alone." She looked confused; her eyebrows furrowed and her mouth hung open, so I repeated the last word silently. I lifted my pointer finger and moved it in a circle. Betrayal etched itself on her face—as if befriending me was betrayal.

Kina's gaze shifted to her brother. "You taught him?"

Raif nodded, then jerked his head for her to go inside. Stepping from the porch, he stood in front of me, signing. *"You need not provoke her."*

A sly grin formed on my lips, crinkling my eyes. "Yet, nothing gives me greater joy." I paused, waiting for a shove, but it never came. Kina was likely inside, listening, so I motioned for Raif to follow. I didn't speak this time—at least not with a voice—I used my hands. *"I need your help."* He pulled back, his hazel-green eyes narrowing suspiciously. *"I'm going after the Hawk, and I need you inside the castle—not in the smith's hole."*

"It's a fool's errand, Nik. You will die in the process. They'd never allow me to step foot into the castle, anyway."

As long as I died after plucking the feathers from the Hawk's hide, I was fine with that. Running my fingers through my hair, I let out a breath through my nose and smiled. "The former may be true, but the latter isn't," I said out loud. "You will be allowed because the crowned princess has requested you."

A soundless curse twisted Raif's features; his eyes

slammed shut as realization dawned on him—he couldn't say no to a royal request. *"What does it entail?"*

I told him exactly what they'd expect of him and by the end, Kina was glaring at the both of us on the porch.

"Do we have a deal?" I asked him, extending my calloused hand toward his.

Nodding, Raif took my hand, clasping it firmly. He took a moment and deliberately crushed it. The pain, as with most pain for me, was dull and uncomfortable—a nagging feeling. I grinned widely at him, to which he only shook his head at me.

He could be frustrated with me all he wanted, Stasya would be safe, as would Edda.

Raif released my hand and turned away, but his hands remained in view. *"Come in and eat."* It wasn't an invitation, it was an order from Raif, which made me chuckle.

"As long as you take away the sharp utensils from Kina, I will dine with you."

Twisting his lips, Raif bared his teeth in a terrifying smile. *"No promises."*

———

By some miracle, I survived breakfast. Raif took a moment to explain to Kina what his new task was, and much to my surprise, the truth of where he'd been lately. The typical underlying fire in her gaze simmered, and she regarded me with raised eyebrows.

"You watch his back, Niklaus, or else I'll hunt you down myself and hold you responsible. I will sell your pale arse to the tanner."

Sighing, I washed the dirty dishes. "I do, Kina. But I'll warn you once, and once only, don't tease me." A deep chuckle escaped me as she pounded her fists into my side. It wasn't a light punch, there was a force behind it, but she also wasn't viciously attacking me. Small steps.

Raif was fortunate to have a sister that understood why he would choose this life—it funded them beyond black-smithing, where they struggled before they visibly were living well. Kina wore a new dress. No dirt clung to the hem yet, no singe marks from the forge were visible. I never could tell Liesel, not that I wanted to. She wouldn't under-stand; she'd even try to convince me that I was perfectly normal.

Drying a plate, Kina murmured, "When does he leave?" She kept her eyes trained on the plate in her grasp, not both-ering to life her gaze.

"As soon as he's ready. The sooner would be better, otherwise, time is being wasted." Finishing the dishes, I leaned against the counter.

Kina placed the last dish into the cabinet, her lips pressed together in a thin line. "Is it true, what Raif said—that you are *her* mate?"

She didn't have to finish the words, but she did. My head snapped up and as much as I wanted to deny it, what was the point? "I didn't tell him that—he assumed—which wasn't a wrong assumption." I expected a scathing remark from Kina, but she surprised me and didn't.

"Then you protect her at all costs. To lose your mate is like losing a part of yourself." Without another word, Kina left the kitchen and disappeared into the hall. The weight of her words hung in the air, and I wondered if perhaps Kina hadn't lost a mate to some tragedy. Maybe one day she'd tell her story, and if not, I would not pry.

A moment later, Raif popped into the room. We shared a look and in return, he nodded his head—Kina knew what it felt like to lose that other half. *"I'll leave in the morning."*

"When you get to the castle, wait for Captain Alric. He'll escort you inside."

"One question." His fingers paused. *"How am I supposed to communicate?"*

"I took care of that for you."

A small smile turned the corners of Raif's lips up. He looked embarrassed. *"Thank you."*

AFTER BREAKFAST we left the comfort of Raif's house. As unsafe as it might have been, we shifted behind his house and took to the woods—it was faster this way, and no need to borrow a horse.

We ran as fast as the woods would allow us to, as fast as the overgrown trees and brush would grant us. When we arrived in the woods that split our paths, we relaxed enough and shifted back.

"Are you sure about this, Nik?" Raif asked.

"For you, yes, for me? No. I'll figure things out as I go."

Raif's nose wrinkled, his dark brows narrowing. *"That is the stupidest idea you've ever had. You need a plan of action to go after that murderess."*

I squeezed his bare shoulder in reassurance. "Step one: you go to the castle. Step two: I piece together and follow the trail the Hawk left behind."

"She won't be an easy target, or clumsy, Nik. She isn't playing around, not to mention this isn't a training mission." He reminded me—as if I needed it.

"I know, and you're right—this is a game to the Hawk—a game she thinks she won and has come to collect her dues. She doesn't know this yet, but she lost. Good luck, Raif."

He nodded his head and shifted into the massive black wolf, then took off toward the castle.

It was time to speak to Sabrina about the hunt.

———

IN THE WOODS BEHIND HEADQUARTERS, I caught a whiff of something strange—it was magic. The electric scent it carried was something I knew well enough. There were stones the Seidel's required us to carry with us on assignments—bloodstones they called them—enchanted gemstones that absorbed the blood of our victims. The stones carried a unique scent to them—as anything with magic did—which was exactly what I smelled now and it only grew stronger.

Not a moment later, Prince Ashroy appeared, his pale hair coiffed at the top, reminding me of a lady groomed for a ball rather than a man. He was far too polished, too pretty, and something about him set me on edge.

Prince Ashroy's crystalline eyes widened in mock surprise and faded quickly. His hand shifted to pocket a gem, or was it an amulet? He was too slow, because my eyes caught the faint glow of the item as he pocketed it.

I arched a brow as he approached, my lips twisting into a knowing smile. What a predicament the two royals had themselves in—Stasya a werewolf and Ashroy a witch. I doubted that Stasya even knew what a witch smelled like. She'd smell the strangeness, but she wouldn't know what it was unless she had been near a witch whilst they were practicing.

"I was hoping I'd catch you before you left," Ashroy began. "I received a letter from one of my contacts, locating the last whereabouts of the Hawk."

More likely than not, Ashroy had used a location spell, which made me wonder, *did the Hawk leave something behind that they could use?* If she had...was it planted? Was she waiting for me?

The prince pressed his lips together and his brows furrowed in question as he waited for me to prod him. "Aren't you curious?"

I stalked forward. "If you think for a moment that I'll beg for a scrap of information from you, you're sadly mistaken. I am not some dog to play with."

"Oh, forgive me." His voice dripped with amusement. "I forgot who I was speaking to." Ashroy moved forward, closing the gap between us. He wore his typical dark blue attire, with the collar of his overcoat brushing his jawline. He looked ridiculous. "I have no intention of playing with you, but I thought for the sake of Princess Stasya, you'd like to know the last location—"

"Why are you here, witch?" I lowered my voice to a whisper, half speaking through my teeth.

Amusement flickered in Ashroy's gaze again, then delight as the truth settled between us. "I need not explain myself to you, but it is common knowledge that I'm here to bond with the princess, and to see if an alliance through marriage is possible. We know of the special circumstances of Her Highness. Ishkertov is a land of opportunity for all kinds. I'm sad to learn that Abendrot is so narrowminded." He sighed, wiping his hands as if to rid himself of filth.

Annoyance crept into my face, creasing my brows and thinning my lips. "Get to the point. If you actually *have* one."

Ashroy swept a hand to the side, and an unnatural silence filled the area. Birds went silent, the wind rustling leaves quieted. Magic hung in the air—I could smell it—and his chilly eyes cooled all the more. He closed the distance between us, narrowing his eyes on me. "I find you humorous, but there is far more at stake than your pride." He sighed, flicking his pale hair away from his eyes. "There is a lead in Brigmoor—there are large barrels and a dock. Something blocks me so I can't see past that, but everything points there. Whether it's a farce, I can't say."

I stiffened. "Brigmoor is on the border of Stalzen." My skin prickled as I said the country's name. Stalzen was a cruel country with wicked practices. It was also a seaport. They had no love for Abendrot and we knew they waited for an excuse to attack. Was the Hawk trying to give them a reason to—A weak and crumbling kingdom, so far in debt that the king's life was taken as compensation?

"How do I know you're not sending me to my death?" I questioned, sidestepping him.

Ashroy pressed his lips together, fighting off a smile. "You don't, but I'm not doing this for you, Niklaus. I am doing this for Stasya and Edda. You could very well drop dead and I wouldn't shed a tear, but I think it would disturb Stasya greatly. Lucky for her—I'm here."

He barely finished his words before I lunged at him, arms extended and ready to pull him down to the marble floor. Yet I never got that far—a barrier formed between us. It felt much like running into a brick wall and it halted my steps immediately. My nose throbbed from where I struck the invisible wall and I could taste the metallic tang of blood.

Ashroy scarcely blinked. "I don't recommend you do that."

Snarling at him, I snapped. "I could say the same for you."

Ashroy shook his head, chuckling. "For all it's worth, I wish you well, Niklaus."

Who could say what side Ashroy played? I knew I couldn't. Whatever awaited me in Brigmoor, I hoped would unveil what this devilish game was. Whether he told the truth was beyond me, but Raif would give it his all trying to protect the royal family. He'd tear Ashroy apart and then some.

There were a few things I had to get in line before I ventured to that hellhole. "You can leave now."

Ashroy waved his hand, dropping the shield. "Finish what you started. Goodbye, Niklaus." With a series of hand gestures, a portal opened in front of Ashroy, and beyond it I could see the walls of the castle. Magic ran as rampantly through the kingdoms as werewolves did. The only difference was I avoided it like the plague.

Never had I seen a portal created, let alone seeing a figure step through and disappear. If he was so magically inclined, why didn't he volunteer his abilities? Growling, I ventured inside to speak to Sabrina.

CHAPTER 6

"We won't let you go there alone and that's that." Sabrina fastened a leather billet on the saddlebag. "We'll move in slowly, so as to not raise suspicion. Be careful in the meantime."

"I will." Settling in on the horse, I sighed. The horse I selected was all black, which made the sight of its white eyes alarming, as did the gleam of its white teeth against the stark black. Riding a horse wasn't on my list of favorite things—creatures of prey loathed wolves—and they knew we weren't human. They could smell it on us, and it spooked them. The horses that the Seidel's kept were crossed with what I suspected was a kelpie. Their thick manes draped across their shoulders, hanging like moss I had seen in swamps. Beneath their forelock their deep black eyes peered out, looking the part of a primeval creature. They were solid and more than a little demonic. If someone told me that blood was part of their daily diet, I wouldn't have been surprised.

"All of you be careful here. Don't let the kingdom fall without me." Winking, I clucked and urged the horse onward.

I rode for a few hours. By the time the sun set, it was time to camp. I knew that sleep would not be visiting tonight, but the horse I dubbed *Demon* needed to rest. I untacked him, fed him, and brushed him down before I got the chance to cram jerky in my mouth.

Nestling against the saddle, my head lolled back, and I gazed up at the stars. Without the sound of a crackling fire I could hear every subtle shift in the vicinity. Normally, an individual would build a fire to keep away predators and for warmth, but I was the biggest predator in these woods. As for extra warmth, I didn't need that, either.

The sound of a quick movement caused me to dart to the side, and a curse fled my lips as I rolled onto my stomach and glared. Demon nearly struck me with his hind leg.

"Do it again, and I'll build a fire just to roast your hide." The horse snorted in reply, which made my eyes narrow. He cast a lazy look in my direction, allowing his head to droop. I swore on some level the horse was mocking me, and considering it belonged to the Seidel menagerie, I didn't doubt it.

Settling against the saddle once again, my mind drifted to Stasya, and I wondered how she was coping with the loss of her father and her new role. Somewhere amidst my musings, I fell asleep.

I awoke to a lashing against my face. Startled, I leaped up, hands reaching to the twin pair of daggers at my hips. Blinking, I found no one in the vicinity, just the annoying beast who snorted and he laughed in his equine fashion.

"I can still make a fire to roast you." Sheathing the blades, the tension in my muscles relaxed. I debated if I should feed the sardonic creature his breakfast, and in the end, he munched away on a bag of oats.

Once the temperamental beast finished eating, I saddled him up. The quicker we made it to Brigmoor the better, and seeing as how we were a few days out, time was of the essence.

———

HALFWAY THROUGH THE DAY, I couldn't seem to shake a growing sense of dread–like this was some trick, sending me to Brigmoor. It weighed on me for a reason I couldn't explain. Why should I panic? Why should I *feel anything?* But I *did.* My gut said this was wrong.

Raif was with Stasya. I trusted him with my life, and I trusted him in the palace, but it was Ashroy and his veiled intentions I didn't trust. I had no other option other than walk into this—trap or not. All I could hope for was that Ashroy truly cared for Stasya and Edda as much as he said.

A few hours later and I'd find a place to stay for the night, to gather my wits, rest, and make a concrete plan.

By morning, I arrived in the quaint town of Kloster. If I thought Walddorf was small, this made my home village seem like a bustling city. Farmlands greeted me, spreading far and wide. I couldn't spot a cottage or shack as far as I could see. It wasn't until Demon and I reached the center of the town that civilization came into view. White homes with red shutters sat in a row, and the storefronts sat amidst them, making it difficult to distinguish which was which. If it weren't for the *Golden Horse Tavern & Inn* sign swinging in the faint breeze, I wouldn't have known the building facing me was, in fact, a place of rest and food.

Beside the Inn was a break in buildings. A small alleyway that led, at least, I assumed, to a stable. I smelled horses, pine shavings, and fresh oats. Hopping down from Demon, I led him down the dark path.

To my surprise, there was an older man already milling around the stable. "Oh, *guten morgen*. T'was not expecting someone so early." He scratched the back of his head and grinned. "Or at all, come to think of it." He cackled, his white, bushy brows furrowing. "What can I do ya for?"

"I need to stable my horse for a day. I don't want you handling him—I'll manage him. Demon can be difficult, and there is no need for you to get hurt." Not bothering to wait for the man to protest, I led Demon into a stall and untacked him. His devilish spirit showed itself, biting my side hard enough to make me yowl. "There is still enough time to eat you," I threatened him.

In reply, he kicked his leg out, narrowly missing me. If I hadn't been pressed against his side, loosening his girth, he would have connected with me. Which, if that happened, I'd be horseless, and fatter by the end of the day.

When I finished tending to the stubborn horse, I paid for his lodging and ventured inside the Inn to deal with mine. There were a few patrons milling around, and by few, I meant three. The establishment was cozy; it reminded me of a grandmother's home. A long wooden table sat next to a fireplace, and two benches inviting whatever patrons were about to sit down. A few single tables nestled against the wall near the entrance, and patrons occupied them.

Above the table, a giant wooden chandelier held more than a dozen candlesticks. Some were half burned down, while others remained unlit entirely. No one looked up from their breakfast as I entered, and only one greeted me.

A portly older woman with graying brown hair

approached me. "*Guten morgen.* Will it be food or lodging for ya?"

"Both. Whatever room you have available will be fine. A day is all I need." As she motioned for me to follow her, I obliged and pulled her payment from my bag.

The woman eyed me curiously, her gaze sweeping up and down my person. "You're not from around here," she noted. "You don't sound like it, anyway. I think I'd remember your face, too. Those freckles, by heavens, your mum must have kissed them senseless when you were little." She shook her head and handed the room key over. "Second door on your left. Will you be havin' stew or our special platter? The platter serves two." She eyed me, as if judging how much I could eat.

"The platter sounds good." I chuckled, nodding my thanks to her as I turned to walk up the hallway. The woman's words brought back fond memories of my mother lathering my face and Liesel's in kisses. It was strange how normal my life had been and here I was now on a mission to kill the Hawk.

———

ALL I NEEDED WAS some breakfast, and a good solid sleep. If I was lucky, I'd sleep an entire day, and I could be on my way tomorrow.

Liesel once told me she dreamed in color, and that her dreams were so vivid that it was as if she were transported to another world. She could taste, smell, and *feel* things as if they were real. I never dreamed. I wasn't sure what it meant, maybe it was a lack of imagination, or perhaps my body needed sleep so desperately that it pulled me into blackness every time.

For once, I dreamed. I dreamed of Stasya nestled in my arms, staring up at me with a smile on her lips. I dreamed of her kissing me, of her whispering sweet promises, and laughing.

A knock on the door pulled me from the dream. Hauling myself out of bed, I shuffled across the floor and blinked as I opened the door. "Yeah?" I rumbled, wiping the sleep from my eyes.

A boy not much younger than me stood off to the side. His clothes were drenched in what I assumed was water, and hay clung to his hair. "Pardon, sir, but it's your horse—"

My reflex was to roll my eyes. "What did he do?"

"He's trying to knock down his stall door."

I cursed. "I'll be right there." There would be no relaxing breakfast. Instead, I gathered a loaf of bread, some dried meat and set off to the stable. When I got there, Demon snorted and rolled his neck before stomping. "Temperamental idiot."

After I cleaned up his mess, I tacked him up and led him outside, mounting him. "Why can't you just behave?" I muttered and spurred him on to continue the rest of our journey.

———

LONG BEFORE WE ARRIVED, I could smell the salty, humid air. The moisture clung to my skin and even gathered on the leather of the saddle and reins. A heavy, thick fog fell over the area, too, snaking in and out of the trees. It made it difficult to see the road ahead, which inspired warm, fuzzy feelings. We rode on. Thankfully, as Demon trotted down a pathway, a signpost confirmed that we were on the right road.

Two hours into the road, there was still no town in sight, but the smell of salt grew stronger, and more individuals frequented the road, which was a good sign. Above, the sun shone as strongly as it could, given winter's hold on it.

When the town finally came into view, so did the heavy scent of fish. Ashroy's words, if they weren't a lie, could be helpful. But how many docks were there in this port town? How many barrels of fish, brews, and other supplies, too? I hoped that my nose would lead me to it.

The port was full of life, including birds that circled the sky in want of an easy catch. They swooped, dove, and danced around the fishermen. When one successfully nabbed a fish, one man lobbed a rock at the bird, narrowly missing it.

Dismounting Demon, I tied him to a hitching post and walked down the dock. I inspected the back of each building, one by one until I saw one with several rows of barrels at the back. Sneaking inside the side door, I pushed my way through, and as soon as I did, my hair stood on end.

A fist collided with my face, then a knee to my stomach, causing me to slump, but I used it to my advantage and barreled into my attacker. Down we went, just in time as a knife whizzed by my head. I glanced up for a moment to see another in the room advancing on us.

"You are at the wrong place, at the wrong time." The man on the floor grinned up at me.

CHAPTER 7

ANGER ERUPTED in the form of my fist connecting with his face. It was a hard-enough hit in the right place that he didn't wake up. The other assailant ran at me with a knife and dove low. Yanking him along, I redirected his movement, and my knee rammed into his stomach. As he twisted to the side, I jerked his arm in an unnatural position and he yowled in pain.

"Where is the Hawk?" I snapped, grabbing up the knife he dropped as he writhed in pain. Hovering over him, I pressed the knife against his throat.

"N-not here." The man laughed in between hissing over his arm. "She never left. You chased the wrong person. I bet right now she's infiltrating the castle."

So it was *her*. This guy was bluffing. He had to be. The blade kissed his skin, pricking it so a trickle of blood seeped out. "You're lying." There was no flinch. No tic, no change in his voice. "The Hawk... is a woman, and the one running this game?" We'd assumed as much, but nothing had confirmed that the assassin who killed Ansgar was the Hawk. Until now, we had been grasping at blades of grass.

I couldn't tell if he was being honest or not. "No. You can believe what you'd like. Abendrot will fall into chaos soon enough, and *she* will reign as queen. You're a fool if you haven't figured out who or what she is by now."

If this was true, Stasya and Edda were in trouble, and I wasn't there. All I could hope for is that Raif would hold his own with the castle guards. Ashroy wasted my time, and I was right to have questioned him. He lied.

In a blink, I slammed the knife down onto the man's good arm, driving it down until it met the floor. "Tell. The. Truth."

He shrieked, an ungodly howl, and bucked beneath me. "I swear. I swear to the gods! She isn't here. I don't know her name. She just calls herself Hawk."

That wasn't what I wanted to hear. "Do you know any witches? Don't lie to me." I twisted the knife in his arm.

He writhed on the ground, paling considerably as the blade twisted in the wound. "Yes! Yes. Manya! She's the one Hawk uses for everything. She lives close by. Stop! I will throw up."

He wasn't lying, at least not about vomiting. I pulled back just as he projectile vomited. "Bring me to her and I won't kill you." I yanked the knife out of his arm and quickly shredded his shirt, using it to bind the bleeding wound. As for his arm, he would have to deal with the sprain.

———

DEMON WASN'T AMUSED that I bound him to the prisoner. "What's your name?" I ground out. He was older than me, that much I could tell. Tawny hair, olive skin. He looked as if he grew up on the docks, but he wasn't a skilled henchman. Or maybe he was only hired for a diversion.

"Urik."

"Urik, are you a fisherman, or do you always fail so miserably at attacking someone?"

He scoffed, lowered his eyes, then said, "She paid well. Fishing has produced little for us. We have no love for the crown, and I thought it'd be easy."

I could understand that. "Fair enough. Where is Manya?" I nodded to the pathway he was leading us to.

"You'll smell it before you see it," he muttered.

His answer had my brows lifting, but sure enough as we continued down the grassy path, a certain stench wafted toward me. It smelled like rotting flesh combined with spoiled seafood. Whatever it was caused the seagulls to cry and dive bomb at the ground.

Movement at the back of the hut caught my attention. A cloak made of what looked to be grass and moss shifted, scattering small songbirds that clung to it. I narrowed my eyes on Urik, willing him to understand if he lied to me, he and this hermit would pay the price.

"Manya," Urik said. "We need you."

Manya shifted, turning to face us, and the eyeless woman smiled. "Do ye now. What have you brought me?"

I kept a firm grip on Urik's back. "I need a portal. Can you do that?"

An eerie, toothless smile curved her lips. "For a price, I can do anything."

Witches were the worst. I loathed everything about them. Their tricks, their stench, and the way they stole things for payment instead of being paid in coin. "Name it and do it quickly."

"A hand."

Urik swore. He fought against the grip I had on him, but Demon's presence behind him kept him from balking entirely. "Are you certain?" I took her silence as confirmation. Unfortunately for Urik, I needed my hands, and the castle needed me more than he needed *his* hand. Without another thought, I unsheathed the long dagger from my hip and severed Urik's hand. It fell to the ground, lifeless and bloody.

There was a moment–a disconnect–between the man and his severed appendage, but when realization–and the pain–dawned on Urik, he shrieked. Not a small yowl, not a sob, but a horrendous wail. He writhed in pain and inevitably he passed out.

Manya kneeled before Urik, murmuring and waving her hand as she sealed the now scarred stump. She greedily picked the hand up and licked her lips. "Very nice. A portal is what you wanted, is it?"

"Yes. Do it quickly." I stepped aside, wiping the bloody dagger on my thigh before sheathing it.

"Thank you, werewolf. Think of where you wish to be." She drew sigils in the air, and in a blink, a portal formed. It was inside the castle's grounds, which would bypass the guards on the outside and make it that much easier for me to rush inside.

Grabbing Demon by the reins, I ran into the portal with him in tow. He bucked, squealed, and tried his best to pull us back to Brigmoor. He didn't succeed; not as I barreled forward. The next breath I took was full of the scent of pine and smoke. A heavy, thick smoke which billowed from the castle's windows.

"No!" I could taste fear on my tongue and feel the dread

coiling in my belly. But with those shoved aside, I ran past the chaos outside and into a burning inferno. Guards and servants ran to douse the flames, scarcely paying me any attention. There were no familiar faces presenting themselves to me, and so I pressed on, running down the grand hall. A familiar scent tickled my nose, one that I knew to belong to Stasya.

A scream rang out. "No! Let me go!"

Stasya. The sound of her voice renewed the urgency within. As I followed her protests, the hallway came to an abrupt end with a wall. I could still hear her, and there were guards posted at the wall.

"Who are you?" One barked.

"Niklaus. I know you know the name. Let me by and you won't get hurt." At least, I assumed he knew the name. I held up a hand as if to say I meant no harm, but should they start a fight, I'd gladly finish it.

"The Big Bad one?" The other guard inquired.

"The same. Now move." I stepped forward, not waiting for them to decide. There was no amusement in my gaze, this was not a game I wanted to play.

The guard closest to me nodded. "We were told if you showed up to let you by. We were told "he" has fiery red hair, devil yellow eyes, and freckles all over. That's you all right." He looked me up and down, his comrade doing the same, and came to the agreement.

As one of them pulled a lever on the wall, it rotated, revealing a hidden stairwell. "Is everyone all right? Are they *all* okay?" They exchanged a look, one I wasn't fond of, and I took that as my cue to bolt down the stairs, ignoring the hollering from behind me.

I could hear Stasya down the winding stairs. It took every fiber in me to not shift, to not blindly run down the stairs and maul whoever had their hands on her. A low, rumbling growl resonated off the walls, then, as I made it to the last stair, I heard Stasya again.

"Niklaus!" she cried, twisting away from the guards who held her. She ran up to me, grabbed my shirt and sobbed. "They took her. They took Edda, and Ashroy. Raif is hurt badly." The words tumbled from her mouth in a frantic mess.

Enveloping her in my arms, I ran my fingers along her back, trying to soothe her. I was furious—they hurt Raif, Edda was gone, but Stasya was safe. I drew in a deep breath, reassuring myself that she was, in fact, in one piece. "I will get Edda back, I swear it."

"And the Prince?" Captain Alric asked. He stepped forward, narrowing his eyes on me.

I hesitated too long. Stasya's forearms shoved into my stomach, her green eyes glaring up at me. She growled. "He tried protecting us, you know. He... He's a witch. But she used this...this thing on him. It looked like a large coin, and the middle was glowing. He couldn't use his magic after that." She looked up at me, puzzled as she spoke of the enchanted item.

I still didn't trust Ashroy. He could have done as much to keep up with his act, playing a victim when all he wanted was to return to his comrade's company. "I will get him back, too." And I made no promises he'd be alive, or in the very least, be alive for long. "She plays with magic. It's how I returned quickly. I found one of her pets, but I wonder if she is magically inclined herself." Motioning to Captain Alric to continue down the secret passage, I continued, "We can discuss this more, but I need to know—where is Raif?"

CHAPTER 8

STASYA PULLED AWAY, flicking a hand to silence the others. "In the barracks. He suffered multiple stab wounds. He is being tended to, but when I last saw him, he was stable." Although she didn't step closer, her hand reached for mine and squeezed it. "I'm sorry. I know he is a friend."

Friend. What did I know of friends? My fingers curled into my palms as we moved down the hall. Raif didn't deserve whatever wounds he received, and it was my selfishness that brought it on. Stasya's fingers brushed against my fist and eased the tension rippling through me.

"It isn't your fault, Niklaus. Raif knew the dangers; he said as much." She placed her other hand around mine, sighing. "Please, whatever you do, don't leave me, not right now." Her grip tightened as we walked down the dimly lit underbelly of the castle.

Captain Alric looked over his shoulder as he walked. "If you're staying with the party, then you must know we are moving Her Highness to Mondwald Castle while the rest sort out through the castle. We don't know how much the fire destroyed." Down the twisting passage he led us until we came to an iron gate that led to stairs. Opening it, he led the way and heaved a wooden door open with the aid of his fellow guard.

Mondwald Castle was part of Abendrot, and just one of the many homes that belonged to the royal family. It was situated amongst the deep forest, because that was where the original family intended to live—amongst the trees and beneath the silvery moon.

"I'll be guarding you tonight, Stasya." The guards grunted at my words, but no more protest than that. I helped Stasya up the steep stairwell, lifting the skirt of her dress so she didn't trip. Horses were already tacked up, and to my surprise, Demon was amongst them. The portal must have disoriented him or panicked him enough to follow a guard.

Stasya walked to a horse and mounted without aid. She fussed with the skirt of her dress, situating it so she could sit astride the horse properly. "You won't find an argument there." She lifted a hand, swiping at fresh tears. "Let's move. Lead the way, Captain."

I mounted Demon, edging him closer to Stasya's horse. "No harm will come to you. I swear it on my life."

Stasya's eyes flicked away after a moment of staring at me. "Don't swear it on your life, Niklaus." She clucked to the horse and followed a trail of guards who took off at a steady pace, leaving me to my curiosities at her cryptic words.

In all the histories ever written, no one had ever explained what went on inside a woman's head or heart. I fully believed that was because *they* didn't even know. As I mulled over her words, something twisted in my chest— a feeling that occurred when I was in Stasya's company. It was more prominent than the call of a bond, and even more confusing.

"One day I'll understand, I guess." Muttering, I prodded Demon into a steady trot to catch up.

As we approached our destination, I realized I had never seen Mondwald Castle before. There were stories and word-of-mouth descriptions, but it was different seeing it in person. A small castle sat sprawling in front of a large pond which reflected the many evergreen trees around, lending it a mossy color. The building itself consisted of red brick and stones, and the window frames were also red, but embellished with ornate trim. I preferred Mondwald Castle to the more imposing one that the royal family occupied.

Our arrival alerted the staff inside. Some individuals ventured outside, intercepting guards, while others ran to perform a task they were ordered to do.

Demon puffed and pawed at the stonework path, sending a loud clang of protest in the immediate area. I dismounted him at the same time Stasya's feet touched the ground. Her back collided with my chest, steadying her. A few hours of riding would do that to anyone—even *my* muscles protested.

"We'll gather our wits, then head out." Captain Alric addressed his men, motioning them toward the entrance of the castle.

I didn't want to admit it, but I needed at least a few hours of sleep. None of the guards were wolves, making them incapable of following a trail by scent alone. The sun would soon set, darkening the woods, making it near impossible for the humans to see without torches. "A few hours isn't going to make or break the situation. I need sleep, and I need it now. If you go out there without me, you will disrupt whatever trail she left. The sun will set soon. I suggest leaving at dawn."

Stasya's lips thinned. An array of emotions played across her face—fear, distress, anger, then resolve. "Don't leave without Niklaus, Captain. You'll need him for what you cannot smell or see. As much as it may pain you, listen to him."

Captain Alric grunted in displeasure, but he bowed his head and closed his fist over his heart. "As you wish, my lady." Alric pulled away, guiding the guards into the castle, which left Stasya and I alone.

"You look terrible." She turned her head, looked up at me and huffed. "When was the last time you slept?" Stasya led the way inside, nodding her head to acknowledge her staff.

We walked to a staircase. An ornate iron railing spiraled upward, leading the way to the upper half of the castle. "Last night." But I'd gone out straight for weeks on end. It was catching up to me. "I just need a little rest. I made a promise to you and I don't intend to break it."

Stasya grabbed my hand and led the way down the hall. She halted in front of a massive oak door and pulled it open. The room, unlike the other castle, was cozy. Although the fireplace wasn't blazing, the dying sun shone inside and cast a warm glow inside. Red, brown, and orange accents in the room reminded me of a warm autumn sunset.

"This is your room?" I asked, already knowing the answer.

"Mhm. It is. Edda and I always shared it. She refuses to stay in her room, even as she's grown." Stasya paused and sat down on the end of the bed. "She always made up stories at bedtime. Tales of adventure, of heroes and villains, dragons, too. They were always so silly, but fun to listen to and would eventually lull me to sleep. She still does it, too." Stasya laughed; a small and half-hearted sound.

I sat next to her and listened. I listened as she talked of Edda, of their youth, and how furious they made one another. I listened as Stasya wept and curled into my side. When she was through, we were both sprawled out on the bed, staring up at the embellished ceiling.

"I'm sorry, Niklaus." Her voice was hoarse. "I'm... I'm lost. I don't know who I'm supposed to be. I know what the country needs, but it wars with who I want to become. I don't know what to do. I want to scream and rage, because I want to be happy, but the country doesn't rely on my happiness; it relies on my duty."

I couldn't fathom what that felt like. I always knew who I was, what I was. But I saw it in Stasya's gaze—she was lost and confused. Who was I to be her guide? What could I possibly have to say that would make a difference?

Slipping my hand along her jaw, I tilted her head back a bit further. In her eyes, I saw vulnerability, and the walls she always hid behind had fallen. "Your country needs a sound leader and not one who wars with herself. You, Stasya, just as you are—that is what your country needs. You understand your people far more than any sovereign has in recent years, and I think you know that. Damn anyone who doesn't believe you should be—"

The next word never left my mouth, because Stasya's lips found mine. She followed my lips as I pulled back, her body moving until it forced her to straddle me. I allowed myself to explore her curves as she melted against me. My tongue dove into her mouth, the taste of her dizzying me. Silver hair spilled from its messy braid and curtained our faces. "Stasya," I murmured between kisses, but she frantically sought them out. "Stasya," I said firmer.

She pulled back, her green eyes glowing. Splashes of red painted her pale cheeks as she stared down at me. "It sounds stupid when I say it out loud, but you are what makes me happy." Stasya whispered against my lips, but she held my gaze. "Do you trust your head more, or your instinct?"

I groaned, letting one hand slide along her back. "You would ask me this while you're straddling me?" She moved her lips to my cheek, ear, and then neck. Stasya's teeth dragged along my neck, and it was then that instinct roared. I swallowed, clutching the fabric of her dress in my hand. "That's a trick question..." A moan replaced my words as she gently bit the skin. "You know as well as I do this isn't a light decision. You can't undo it." But that damnable instinct said otherwise. It wanted this as badly as Stasya did.

"I don't want to undo it, Niklaus. As it is, it drives me mad. Every time I send you away, a piece of me snaps, which I know is insane!" She cupped my face with both her hands and lowered her lips to mine. "When I said I hate you, it wasn't *you*. I hate this feeling, because I don't know you, and it's strong enough to scare me. I know you're always there, though. You've saved me, you tease me, and in some bizarre way you encourage me. I want to know you. I want to know more of where you came from, what your mother was like. I want you."

It was my turn to silence her with a kiss. As my lips covered hers, our limbs tangled and my hands hovered over the stays of her dress. "What is your choice?"

Smiling down at me, she tugged at my shirt. "I need you, and I want *this* right now. I need something to distract me from running blindly into danger, because I will." Stasya bent her head and kissed my throat, then the tender spot just beneath my ear. "And what is your choice?"

"I don't know if I ever had one. I think the gods chose for me when our paths crossed. Even so, I'd choose you." I chuckled, then hissed as Stasya's teeth broke through my skin. At once my eyes flashed a brilliant hue of yellow. A familiar feeling snaked through me, waiting for me to make a move. I pulled Stasya down toward me, kissed and teased the spot below her ear, then bit down. The bond snapped into place, and with it came a torrent of *feelings* that weren't mine. It was a heady sensation that rippled through me, spurring my actions on, begging for me to complete the centuries old ritual of a bond.

In a flurry of movements, we threw aside our clothing and our limbs tangled further. Both of us surrendered to our instinct and gave in to what nature intended for us—to be mated.

Afterward, Stasya lay curled up in my arms, and I allowed for my body to fall into a deep, much needed slumber.

———

WHEN I WOKE, Stasya's back faced me, silver spun hair draped over her shoulder and spilled onto the bed. As much as I didn't want to leave, I knew I had to. I also knew that I had to leave before she roused, or else she would demand to come with me. That couldn't happen—Stasya couldn't be put in harm's way again.

I watched as she slept, experiencing a nagging need to place a kiss to her neck, and yet I knew if I did, she'd wake. The promise I made I intended to keep, bring Edda back at all costs, but I wasn't foolish enough to promise my return. I *was* stupid enough to mate with her, which meant if I died, what would happen to Stasya?

I couldn't think about it. I wouldn't allow myself to.

Once dressed, I headed downstairs. It was time to speak with Captain Honorable–Alric–about our plan.

CHAPTER 9

EARLY DAWN LIGHT trickled through the windows of the castle, casting a blue light on everything it touched. Judging by the moon's placement, and the faint glow of the sun on the horizon, I'd slept over four hours.

I needed to get moving—we all needed to.

A few groggy faces turned to glance up at me when I entered the common room. Their chattering paused, then continued as I walked up to Alric. "Did you brainstorm while I slept?" I murmured.

"Some—not all—slept. We didn't get very far with a plan." Alric stood from his seat. Bags hung beneath his eyes, and while I had no love for him, I could say I respected him a little more through this ordeal.

I nodded, running a hand along my chin. "Tracking the Hawk isn't an easy task. I've discovered she uses magic, but not her own. At least, she hasn't used her own thus far. There is a distinct smell in the air when a magic user practices—like sulfur and smoke—which hasn't been present whenever magic has shown up in her wake." I walked over to the fireplace, which had a small fire blazing in it.

"Tell us everything you know, Niklaus." Alric stepped toward the hearth and sighed. "We need all the help we can get."

So I told him everything I knew—of how the woman was using people in Brigmoor, of how I came to confirm it was, in fact, a woman and the same one who killed Ansgar. I told them what the Hawk wanted: a kingdom that was owed to her.

"What?" Alric sunk onto an ottoman next to the fireplace. "How? Why would King Ansgar promise a kingdom to such a wretch? Why would he do that to us?"

I leaned my forehead against the mantel, sighing. "Desperation causes people to do the most peculiar things, don't you think? Abendrot is indebted to this woman. Whoever she truly is, she bought Abendrot when the king so foolishly sought her help. The only way the *contract* is null and void is if she is killed. After that, it's a matter of cleaning up her crumbs in Brigmoor, and wherever else she has poisoned."

Alric's hands covered his face as he swore loudly. "If we fail..."

I laughed at his words—a genuine laugh which made my shoulders quake. "If we fail, we're dead and it won't matter, but don't plan on failing, plan on winning and gutting the bird. You have Edda and Stasya counting on you. Now, let's discuss where we'll be searching."

I think by the end our discussion Alric hated me a little less and perhaps respected me a little more.

———

WE SPLIT OUR PARTIES UP; I was with Alric, and his second in command was with the other group. Hours were between the abduction and us heading out, but there weren't many main roads in Abendrot—there were two, and all the others intersected with them.

Instead of riding, I opted to walk on foot, but Demon was still tacked up and ready for me. He wasn't keen on being ponied by another guard as we traipsed through the woods, but he didn't have a choice. I needed him ready just in case I had to hop on him.

The sun's growing strength in the sky provided better lighting for the humans behind me. It enhanced my sight but wasn't necessary. I could smell traces of Ashroy's magic, which meant he had been using it. I didn't trust that he'd been trying to protect Stasya and Edda. I fully believed he was using it to trick them.

"Wait." I knelt on the edge of the path, inspecting the ground where a discard glove lay. I sniffed it–it was Edda. Was I supposed to trust this? Or was it a trap laid out to ensnare me?

Alric halted the party. "What is it?" He squinted as he looked at the ground, trying to decipher what I had.

"A glove. It has Edda's scent all over it. I don't know if I trust this—it can't be this easy." Looking down the path, I sighed and continued to walk on.

An hour down the road and small farms dotted the landscape. Instead of being suffocated by tall pines, the land opened into rolling hills and fields. Morning dew hung heavily in the air, smelling of sweet ozone. And blood. Where was the smell of blood coming from?

My heart pumped wildly, but panic didn't course through me. I jogged down a row of dried cornstalks. The sound of horses trampling them behind me ruined the tranquil silence of the farmlands.

"What do you have?" Alric spoke up. "What is it?"

I didn't answer him. I ran across the cornfield until I found a spot of blood with a note pinned to it by a dagger. It wasn't Edda's—there was nothing of her scent wafting from it—but the note also told me who it belonged to.

DEAREST HUNTER,

I trust you're enjoying this game of hide and seek. You're closer than you think and because of that, here is a splash of Ishkertov's finest brew. The blood of a prince is worth quite a lot, as is a princess'. How much are they worth to you? Would you die for them?

I look forward to your answer.

Kind regards,

The Hawk

HALF of the blood had dried, but some of it was still wet, which meant I truly wasn't that far behind. My face flushed with annoyance.

"It's not Edda's. It's Ashroy, and we're almost there. Be on alert, I don't like this. I believe it's a setup."

A howl in the distance caught me off guard. I twisted around as I stood and swore. I approached the guards. "Ride as fast as you can back from where we came from." My eyes widened, chest rising and falling quickly.

"Why? What the hell is going on, Niklaus?" Alric barked.

"Stasya." I felt it. I understood the stories of the bonding that took place. I knew the howl, but I felt it in my chest. The panic that belonged to her, the desperation, and it unsettled me. "I don't care how you make sure she doesn't get here, just do it. If you have to knock her out, do it." She howled again in the distance. This time, rage twisted it, causing it to sound more like a shriek.

The guards looked uncomfortable, twisting in their saddles. But to my surprise, it was Alric who spoke up. "Do as he says. We cannot afford to lose the princess." He turned to me and nodded his head. "I'll stay with you; the rest can *go*." He growled the last word, and promptly the rest galloped off, with Demon in tow. "Whatever you're about to do, do it fast. If they can't hold her off in wolf form... she's coming straight for you."

"Go join them, Alric. Go!" Without a glance, Alric took off to find the others. Another howl rang out, but this time it wasn't Stasya. Alric didn't know that, and that was just as well. This wolf was closer, just beyond the wood line. "Who are you?" I whispered. Then, I ran with everything I had across the field. In the distance, I heard a whispering, faint as the breeze.

"I am here. I am here. I came for you," the voice repeated itself.

I knew that voice. I knew who had followed me, and the only one who owed me nothing. "Stay there. Protect her... Please." I wasn't above begging at this point. "No matter what, stay with her."

I heard it before I felt it, just as I was about to crash into the woods—an arrow embedded itself into my shoulder, slamming me backward. I collided with the ground, falling heavily onto my back. It knocked the wind from me, and I groaned, yanking the arrow out.

A wolf's shriek echoed in the woods. Gnashing my teeth together, I stood to my feet, ignoring the cries from Stasya.

"Coward—hiding in the woods—show yourself. I know you're there, and I'm done playing games."

"Oh, all right, hunter. You've been fun to play with." The hawk stepped from the woods, dressed in black garb. Her long coat billowed in the gentle breeze, and her face lacked any covering. A middle-aged woman stood before me —an olive-skinned beauty. Her full red lips quirked into a salacious smile, and her almond eyes were as black as night. She was absolutely stunning. "If circumstances were different, I think we'd have a different game to play."

"No."

"Really?" She stepped closer, plucking black gloves from her hands. "I don't believe you. Tell me, hunter, do you know what Lethe is?"

I glanced down at the arrow on the ground and my heart slowed. "You poisoned me." Despite the situation, I grinned. "I was right. You are a coward."

"Oh, don't be dramatic. Lethe will plunge you into a sleep and ease your memories."

Ease my memories. That was code for forgetting. "No. I won't forget." I lunged for her. Even though my limbs protested, I fought against the sluggishness that threatened to take over.

I grabbed her hair, twined it around my hand and yanked her to the side, but she expected my movements. With ease, she twisted around. Her fingers launched forward and found the newly made hole. I howled in pain, willing myself not to let go, but she pressed her fingers in deeper. When I collapsed to the ground, she whipped out a leather cord and wrapped it around my neck, choking off my air supply.

"I wonder, what would your princess do to save your life?" she whispered in my ear. Her lips brushed against my hairline even as I struggled. The more I struggled, the heavier my body grew.

I slid my fingers under the throng, gasping for fresh air. Distant shouts filled the air, growling and snarling. The throng around my neck loosened a fraction, and I yanked as hard as I could. The woman lost her balance, but as she righted herself, she landed a solid kick to my jaw. I instantly tasted blood; it dripped from my mouth onto the ground.

"I'll give you this, you're a stubborn one. Go to sleep and when you wake you won't remember a damn thing." Her patience thinned. It was clear in her crisp tone—the seductive, playful edge had disappeared.

I laughed, regretting it at once as my jaw throbbed. "I won't make your job easier." I rolled to my fours and swayed. In the distance, the growls in the woods turned to human whispers. I doubted the woman could hear them. They were hushed, and it made me smile. "Do your worst to *me*." Fred wasn't about to let Stasya go, and with the guards behind them, the Hawk had no option but to flee, with or without me. Pain lanced through my chest in the form of emotions that weren't mine.

Amusement turned my lips upward, much to the Hawk's dismay. She didn't know the Huntsmen were following me. The last thing I saw was a boot flying toward my face. I fell into a black void in slow motion.

CHAPTER 10

FIRE ENCOMPASSED MY SHOULDER; it felt like Liesel had taken a hot poker and stuck me with it. Groaning, I sat up. Dizziness overcame me, and my stomach flipped. "Li... are you down there?" I called. "Are you in the kitchen?" I didn't dare open my eyes yet.

There was movement in the room, the sound of shuffling and a scoff before it came closer to me. "You love your big—"

"I will stop you right there. I don't have a clue what your fantasy is about, but I won't let you continue it with me. You need to wake up, Niklaus. Wake up!" A *thwack* sounded as the individual smacked me hard across the face.

That wasn't Liesel. My eyes opened, and I sprung out of bed, stumbling as I clutched onto the other's shirt. My limbs didn't want to cooperate. "Who... are you?"

A curse escaped from the other. "Ashroy. You were poisoned with Lethe. I don't know how long we have but shut up and listen to me."

"Where is Liesel?" I mumbled, growing agitated. I glanced around—I was in a cell. Why the hell was I inside a cell, and with this blond twit?

"I don't know who Liesel is, but I will assume she's where you left her." Ashroy sighed, settling me back down on the bed. "Lethe is designed to make you forget." His eyes darted to my neck, which unbeknownst to me, still had the fresh marks from a mating. "It's not my place to inquire about your... dalliances. However, it seems you've recently," he paused, pinching the bridge of his nose. Dropping his hand, he motioned to my neck. "You've mated with someone, and I'm fairly certain I know who that someone is. Which means, that idiotic move could be your—our—saving grace. You're bonded to *her*, which means the memories which are allegedly forgotten, will be easier to dig up. Poison can't erase memories, not really. Only magic can truly erase, and the Hawk didn't use magic."

Confusion furrowed my brow, caused my head to ache, and all I wanted was to sleep. But as this Ashroy spoke, I felt the ache in my chest, and a swirl of emotions. I didn't *have* emotions. "How do you know magic wasn't used?"

Ashroy's pale eyebrows lifted. "Because when you were carted in they were snickering about it. Aside from that? A witch always know." He sighed and threaded his fingers through his messy hair. "Tell me you had a plan. Gods, you don't even remember. Why am I asking you?" Ashroy stood up and kicked a tray of what was supposed to be food. That watered-down stew looked more like tripe than anything.

"Ashroy, are you okay?" a small voice called out, belonging to a girl. She rustled in the cell next to us and peered through the bars. "Oh, Niklaus! You're here? Is Stasya okay? Are you okay?" A torrent of questions escaped her.

She reminded me of Liesel, with wild red hair and vibrant eyes. That girl didn't belong in a cell. That girl looked a lot like the youngest princess. "Why are you in here? And Stasya—as in the princess? Why wouldn't she be okay?"

I moved from the bed and toward the iron bars, peering at the girl's tear-stained face. "Did someone hurt you?" I narrowed my eyes.

"Edda, he doesn't remember. It'll come back, darling," Ashroy spoke up.

A sob wracked the girl's shoulders. She leaned her forehead against the bars and gave in to a fit of tears. "You were supposed to save us."

My head throbbed, and I felt as though I were in a nightmare, unable to wake. Nothing made sense! My head ached, and the more I tried to remember, the more it throbbed. "If that's the case, then you can expect I'll do just that." I murmured, and reached through the bars, brushing away her tears. The similarity between Edda and Liesel was uncanny, and I couldn't help but want to soothe her. "I guess that's what I'll do then. I'm not above gutting someone in order to get out of here."

Hope glistened in Edda's eyes. "Really?"

"Oh yes, really." I winked and motioned for her to go settle down. "Go get some rest, I will talk to Ashroy." I turned to face him, folding my arms. "Tell me everything you know."

Ashroy's crystal gaze hardened. "Everything? That will take a while."

Looking around our cell, I chuckled. "Doesn't look like we'll be going anywhere, anytime soon. So, yeah, *Assroy*, everything."

He rolled his eyes, then rubbed his face tiredly. "Are you sure you don't remember anything?" Ashroy scoffed before he relayed everything he knew. Right up until the Hawk abducted them, which was apparently yesterday.

My head throbbed, because as much as I didn't want to believe him, it made sense. "But you knew when you came to Abendrot that Ansgar had sold it? You knew it was in danger."

"We knew. We knew more or less it was Lady Domitia— or as you've known her—the Hawk. Not all her fellow birds are true to her and had word she sought a kingdom to start a war with. Prior to being named the Hawk, she was once amongst every high court in the continent. Rumors said she was on the verge of pushing for an empire, and with the position of bed mate to one of the continent's richest kings... it was possible."

Angrily, I rubbed my head, willing myself to remember what I forgot. "She would start with Abendrot, and do what?"

"Likely offer it as a present and promise to King Lianus to show how capable she is."

Sartana was an ocean away. It should have presented little to no threat. Yet here we were. "You're a witch. Why didn't you zap her or something?"

Ashroy's shoulders shook with amusement and he groaned. "I would have *zapped* her if she didn't possess wards to block it. Lethe isn't the only poison she carries, and she drugged me long enough to place this on me." He pointed to the iron choker around his neck. "It blocks me."

Nausea brought me to my knees, and I vomited until nothing was left. Afterwards, I curled up on the poor excuse for a bed. "I will kill her." They were the last words I muttered before darkness claimed me again.

"RISE AND SHINE, my beautiful hunter. I have an opportunity for you." Lady Domitia opened the cell door and motioned for me. I had no choice but to follow and see what game she wanted to play. "I had a bath drawn for you, and I found new clothes, too." She led me down the dank hallway, to the stairwell and up to the first floor.

I had never seen a house this elaborate before—or maybe I had—I didn't remember. Velvet drapes shielded the harsh sun, which I was grateful for. I didn't think my eyes could handle anything more than darkness. Crystal chandeliers hung from the ceiling and held several stubbed-out candles. Lady Domitia was as rich as she was clever.

"In here. I'll be waiting for you, so hurry." She opened the door to a guest room, inside smelled of pine and citrus. It tickled my nose.

I lifted my brows and stepped in, closing the door behind me. I direly needed a bath, and maybe it'd clear my head.

Halfway through scrubbing the dirt away, a knock came. "Hurry, dearest. We have much to discuss."

I lobbed the bar of soap at the door and heard a laugh. However, I hurried and dressed in the loose white shirt she picked, and dress slacks. Curling my lip, I pulled my boots on and stepped from the room, only to be face to face with Domitia.

"Much better," she cooed and motioned for me to follow.

The scent of cooked food caused my stomach to protest. I wanted to eat, but I wanted no gifts from her. Inwardly, I groaned as the table came into view. The dining hall was set up for a banquet, but it was just the two of us.

Domitia sat at the head of the table, and I sat next to her.

She placed her hand on top of mine and smiled wickedly. "I have a proposition for you and considering you're on the losing side, choose wisely." She paused as I snatched my hand away.

"Domitia, that's no way to seduce a young man to do your bidding," I hissed and folded my arms.

Fine eyebrows lifted in delight as she leaned forward. "So, Ashroy told you. I should have known." She laughed as she stood, then leaned against the arm of my chair. "Dearest, if I wanted to seduce you, I wouldn't need words. Listen closely: either join me and my ranks, or you can die with the rest of the royal family in Abendrot."

Every muscle tensed, wanting to shift, wanting to tear her into shreds, but the poison still fogged my mind. I couldn't feel a large part of myself. I snarled at her. "Humor me, Domitia, what exactly are your ranks?"

She leaned forward and brushed her lips against the tip of my ear. "An empire."

ACKNOWLEDGMENTS

First of all, thank you for reading this installment of The Hunter series! Without you, this would just be a sad, lost story amongst the sea of stories out there. So, I thank you from the bottom of my heart. It truly means the world to me.

I want to take a moment to thank the team of individuals who had a part in helping this story come to life.

K.M. Robinson, thank you for always being my go-to for help. No matter *what* it is, you're there!

Also, Yentl, I love you x3000! Your cheerleading and support means the world to me. When I need a confidence boost or a kick in the pants, you're my girl. I'd marry you in a heartbeat.

Ashley and Val, you girls are the best. Honestly, you take the brunt of my dramatics when it comes to writing. I love you girls, and can't thank you enough for listening to my plot ramblings, or insecurities! Because who actually knows how to write?!

I want to thank Melanie Gilbert for being a writing partner, and also being there to listen to my ramblings as well as writer complaints. I'm so glad I have you in my life.

A huge shout out to my children, Toryn and Evelyn, you two are my super stars. Thank you for understanding mummy needs her quiet time to write. When God was handing out kiddos, I hit the jackpot with you two.

ABOUT THE AUTHOR

Elle was born and raised in Southeastern, Massachusetts in a little farm town by the harbor. She grew up fascinated with all things whimsical and a strong love for animals. As she grew so did her passion for reading and writing. Although she prefers devouring all genres she largely enjoys dark fantasy.

She is married to her best friend and has two lively sprites who inspire madness, love and a sense of humor in her. They also have a menagerie of animals, two dogs, three cats and a horse. In her downtime, Elle enjoys creating candles, crocheting, horseback riding and running.

facebook.com/ellebeaumontbooks

twitter.com/ellebeaumont

instagram.com/ellebeaumontbooks

ELLE BEAUMONT'S NEWSLETTER

Did you know that by signing up for my newsletter you get first access to deals, events, behind the scenes, giveaways, and you receive FREE books?

Sign up for free goodies today or you can visit ellebeaumontbooks.com for more information.

ASSASSIN'S GAMBIT PLAYLIST

You can find the complete "Hunter's Truce" playlist on Spotify by searching for Elle Beaumont.

1. Man on a Mission by Oh The Larceny
2. Hellfire by Barns Courtney
3. Used to the Darkness by Des Rocs
4. Twisted by MISSIO
5. Glitter & Gold by Barns Courtney
6. Call Me Devil by Friends in Tokyo
7. Bury Me Face Down by grandson
8. Cold Blood by Dave Not Dave

MORE FROM ELLE BEAUMONT

The Hunter Series

Hunter's Truce

Royal's Vow

Assassin's Gambit

Queen's Edge [available 5/5/2020]

Veiled Allurement: A Cinderella Retelling Novella

Baron Weaver Series

Game of Bezique

Secrets of Galathea Collection

Brotherhood

Bindings

Voice

King

MORE BOOKS YOU'LL LOVE

If you enjoyed this story, please consider leaving a review!

Then check out more books from Crescent Sea Publishing!

WHEN STARS ARE BRIGHT BY AMBER R. DUELL

For Lina Holt, a Dutch seventeen-year-old with a flair for singing, 1930 is going to be her year. Her long-time boyfriend is about to propose and her mother will finally realize their relationship isn't a passing phase. But when a stranger snatches her from her backyard, everything changes.

Lina is thrust into the spotlight of a New York vaudeville show where she's paired with Nik, a mysterious pianist. The two bond during rehearsals and it doesn't take long before Nik puts himself at risk to confess a hidden truth. Without Lina, the show is in its last season and there's no way she'll be allowed to slip through the owner's fingers. Not when she carries fairy magic in her blood—an gift that turns her song into a dangerously addictive drug.

If Lina ever wants to return home, she must learn who to trust before she's forced to remain a prisoner on stage forever.

MULAN DRAGON SHIFTER BY K.M. ROBINSON

**There are no female dragon shifters in Yan Liu…
except Mulan and her family.**Only the enemy province has women with scales, so when they attack the Center as Mulan is dropping off her twin brother for his assignment with the army, she's forced to play the role of a non-existent brother after she shifts and rushes into the battle to protect her real twin.

Together, they must lie to their commanding officer—Mulan's secret boyfriend—and the entire army to protect her from their wrath should they find out and consider her an enemy, but Mulan's special gift might be too great to keep her secret hidden for long. She may be the only one that can save the kingdom and return the black jade blossom to the emperor.

Can Mulan survive the war, navigate two men vying for her attention, and keep her scales hidden long enough to return the province's life source to her people, or will dark, hidden forces destroy everything and cause her plans to burn hotter than her scale-melting dragon flames?

9 781948 668514